I0450783

RETURN OF THE RED

Red Tail Trilogy Book 1

RAGAN CARMICHAEL

Lavish
Publishing LLC

This book is a work of fiction. The characters, incidents, and dialogue are drawn from the author's imagination and are not to be construed as real. Any resemblance to actual events or persons, living or dead, is entirely coincidental.

RETURN OF THE RED Copyright 2025 ©

All rights reserved under International and Pan-American Copyright Conventions. By payment of the required fees, you have been granted the non-exclusive, non-transferable right to access and read the text of this e-book on-screen. No part of this text may be reproduced, transmitted, down-loaded, decompiled, reverse engineered, or stored in or introduced into any information storage and retrieval system, in any form or by any means, whether electronic or mechanical, now known or hereinafter invented, without the express written permission of Lavish Publishing, LLC.

First Edition

Red Tail Trilogy Book 1

2025 Lavish Publishing, LLC

All Rights Reserved

Published in the United States by Lavish Publishing, LLC, Midland, Texas

Cover Design by: Victor R. Sosa

Cover Images: Depositphotos

Paperback edition

ISBN: 978-1-944985-98-1

Contents

Chapter One

Mac

A pebble dug into the flesh of her cheek. She was supposed to be asleep in her sleeping bag with her head on her bunched-up sweatshirt. Her hands tingled and she shivered from the cold seeping into her body from the stone floor. Blinking to clear her vision, she wondered how she came to be here. She wrinkled her nose at the slight smell of a kennel. It had been cleaned but the stink of feces remained.

Sitting up, her head whirled and she instinctively tried to bring her hand up to her forehead to rub at the ache but her hands were tied behind her back, the rope feeling hot against the flesh of her wrists. Her mind was curiously blank. Blank? Where was her Wolf? The silence in her head scared her more than her present predicament. She probed around in her head, relief flooding through her when she felt the familiar tickle of her Wolf awakening.

The last she remembered she'd been in Wolf form, joyous at the freedom of running through the forest with the wind in her fur. She flexed her arms, wincing at a twinge in her shoulder, wondering what had caused the twinge. So used to the quick healing afforded to her by her were blood, she was surprised at the pain. From the chills wracking her body, she must have been lying on the stone floor for hours for the cold to have reduced her normally high body temperature. That should have been plenty of time to heal even the most grievous of wounds.

And where was her bra? She was wearing the jeans and t-shirt she'd left folded neatly on a large rock in the woods but not the brand-new bra she'd paid too much money for. And where were her boots? Twisting, she scanned the room, looking for her belongings. The disorientation came over her in waves, making her want to be sick. What the hell had happened?

The screech of rusty hinges behind her had her squirming to turn and face the door. She looked up into a face she did not know, her Wolf growling.

"Wolf," she heard in her mind.

She looked at the man in surprise. In all of her travels she'd never met another Wolf face to face. She'd seen others from a distance but this was the first she'd actually been close enough to smell. He had a not unpleasant musky smell. Was that how she smelled to others?

"Why am I here?" she asked, the quaver in her voice concerning. The ropes wrapped around her wrists and ankles tingled against her skin, the tingling radiating through her body.

"What pack?" he growled.

She shivered at his stare; his eyes boring into the deepest recesses of her mind searching for who knows what. "Pack? I don't have a backpack."

He frowned and walked behind her and lifted her up onto

her feet by her right arm. Grasping the neck of her shirt, he pulled the back down, the material digging into her throat. "Where's your tattoo?"

"Hey," she gasped as he pulled the shirt down further, exposing her back.

His fingers touched the skin on her right shoulder blade, then her left.

"Where's your pack tattoo?"

So, he meant a pack like a group, not her backpack. "I don't have a pack," she replied. Wondering why a pack was such a big deal.

"So, you're a Rogue," he stated as he pulled her shirt back up. "Let's go, the Alpha wants to see you."

"The Alpha?" she queried, wondering what the hell this guy was talking about.

She watched as he pulled on a pair of gloves. Her stomach twisted when he tugged a large leather dog collar off a hook near the door.

"No way you're putting that on me," she rasped, her throat dry from fear. Her struggles made him smile.

"Even with the wolfsbane you're still a spitfire. Maybe I'll petition the Alpha for you. I'm looking for a strong mate."

"No mate," her wolf growled, stronger, fighting the effects of whatever they'd dosed her with. "Cocky asshole."

She almost laughed out loud. Her wolf had that right, he was a cocky asshole. Her skin burned when he placed the collar around her neck. No wonder he'd put gloves on, the burning increased until she swore she could smell cooking meat. She panted through the pain, surprised when she heard him snap a leash onto the collar.

"This really isn't necessary. Why don't you take off the collar and we can talk about this?"

He stared at her. "Standard procedure for Wolves who

trespass on Black Paw land." He pulled a knife out of his pocket and bent down to cut at the rope around her ankles.

"Black Paw? What's that?"

He stood as he closed the knife and pocketed it. Transferring the leash to his right hand, he pushed her forward, "Let's go, the Alpha doesn't like to be kept waiting."

"Who or what is the Alpha?"

"Quiet," he snarled. "You'll find out soon enough."

Her legs still tingled, the after effect of the ropes. A whimper followed them down the hall, making her wolf whine. "Pup," her wolf howled in her head as she trotted after her jailor. "Have to help."

Stumbling, she forced herself to keep walking. Six doors along the corridor, why did they need so many cells? Her attention on the doors behind them, she bumped into her jailor when he stopped and placed his hand on a plate affixed to the wall. With a click the door swung open, and he pulled on the leash, forcing her forward.

Brock

Brock watched from where he leaned against the wall as Jase walked into the throne room, a leash in his hand hooked to a collar around a woman's neck. His wolf growled, *"Asshole."* Tamping down his wolf's anger, he reminded him they didn't have the authority to question the going's on in the Black Paw Pack. Not yet. He couldn't jeopardize his cover as a Rogue looking for a pack. Stories about Black Paw had been circulating ever since the old pack leader had died with no clear heir. Dennis Gladieaux, a fairly new member originally from Louisiana, had claimed leadership, killing the Beta wolf in a challenge as allowed by Wolf law. Taking over the pack, he ruled with intimidation and fear. Rumor had it he was building an army to take over the top spot in the Wolf hierarchy.

Brock continued to lean against the wall, his stance showing disinterest in the proceedings as his Wolf whined. Behind his mirrored sunglasses his eyes took in everything from the asshole slouched in the elaborately carved chair up on a dais, his leg thrown over the arm, boredom evident on his face, to the girl facing him, her pink hair a bright spot in the room.

"Mine," his Wolf growled as he stared at the pink-haired female.

"Shhh, no time for fun," he thought back.

"Not fun, fated," his Wolf growled back.

Sent here by The Alpha of the Red Tail Pack, the North American leader of all Wolves, Brock's job was to gather evidence of the growing unrest, not to look for a mate. His arms crossed, he balled his right hand into a fist, his nails digging into the flesh of his palm to keep his temper from showing. Mistreatment of females always got his Wolf riled up.

The woman stumbled behind Jase; her hands bound in back of her. He could feel the pain rolling off her, the silent cries of her Wolf tearing at him. His Wolf sniffed, growling at the slight scent of wolfsbane. Dammit, they must have soaked the ropes in it to keep her under control. The use of wolfsbane was outlawed except in the most severe cases. Another mark against this guy.

Back straight, the girl stood tall and faced the throne. Throne, God this guy was a piece of work. His hands itched to wrap around his throat and squeeze. The Weres around him looked at the floor, not making eye contact, fear evident in their body language.

Jase cleared his throat. "She has no tattoo and won't tell me her pack affiliation."

The Alpha sat up, as if something about the girl had caught his attention.

"You were found in your Wolf-form on Black Paw land without permission. Why?" he sneered at the girl.

Flipping her pink hair out of her eyes with a snap of her head, she stared him in the eye. "How was I supposed to know. Nothing was posted."

Brock was intrigued by her bravery, not many Wolves would be able to look this ass in the eye without flinching. He moved closer to the girl.

"Silly girl, has no one taught you Wolf etiquette? You always announce yourself to the local pack before going on a run. What should I do with you?"

Still looking him in the eye, she replied. "Let me go. I'll leave and you'll never have to see me again."

He stared at the ceiling in exasperation. "How will that teach you anything?" He stood and stretched. Flipping his hand at Jase he said, "Take her back to her cell and teach her some manners." He sauntered to the edge of the dais. "And make her tell you her affiliations. Obviously, her pack needs some lessons in Wolf law."

Brock stood and strolled to the girl, removing his sunglasses to look her over. "Let me. I find I'm interested in this little pink-haired female. She looks like she might be fun in bed."

The Alpha turned and looked at him. "This skinny thing? To each his own." He stroked his close-cut beard. "To celebrate you pledging your fealty at the ceremony this evening, I'll give her to you as a mate. She's yours, Asher. Don't come back until you have the information I want from her."

Brock held out his hand, curling his fingers around the

end of the leash when Jase placed it on his palm. "I'll get the information," he said with a wicked grin.

Turning, he tugged on the leash, his stomach twisting as the girl turned to follow him. He had to get her out of the room before his Wolf went berserk. Fated mates were rare and if she truly was his fated mate, his Wolf would stop at nothing to protect her.

Chapter Two

Mac

She stumbled behind the guy in the sunglasses, her head up staring at his back as if that would help her gauge his mood. He was much scarier than the pompous idiot who acted like he was a king. Seriously, that guy was slimy, but she could handle him. This guy, on the other hand, scared her. His face hard as granite, she wished she could see behind the mirrored lenses on his face. She wanted to run but there was no way she'd get the leash away from him. How could that pompous ass give her away like a piece of his property? Just the thought of it made her want to puke.

When he looked back at her, his control slipped, surprise showing on his face for a second before the mask slipped back into place. Throwing open a door he pulled her out into the bright light of day. Holy crap, it looked like it was at least four in the afternoon, she'd been unconscious on that stone floor for hours and now her muscles were starting to protest.

Tugging on the leash he growled at her. "Move it. I don't have all day."

When she tripped, he stopped and picked her up and put her over his shoulder in a fireman's carry. "Fuck, how long did they let you lie there tied up in ropes soaked in wolfsbane?" he muttered.

His steps jarred her, even though she could tell he was trying to walk softly. What was up with this guy? As she bounced on his shoulder she looked around, trying to orient herself. She recognized the building they'd exited as the auditorium she'd passed the day before. That meant they were in Ankton, about thirty miles outside of Fort Wayne. If she could get away from this guy, she could get out of town. Disappear.

The collar burned against her neck, making her wonder about wolfsbane. What was it? And how had she not known there were Weres nearby? Over the years she'd become better at spotting her own kind, staying clear of them. Maybe it was the prospect of a run in the woods that had distracted her. Now it seemed she was in some deep shit.

The Wolf carrying her put her on her feet in front of a small house on the outskirts of town. Once they were inside and he'd slammed the door behind them he pulled out a pocketknife and started sawing at the ropes around her wrists. She watched as his mouth got tight when she hissed at the stinging from the wolfsbane.

Finally, the ropes parted and her arms were free. Lightly rubbing her fingers over her wrists, she looked in horror at the deep red welts marring the flesh.

Dropping the knife on the floor, he reached for the buckle on the collar. "Fuck," he muttered when he got it undone and it dropped away. "I've got something that will help with the burning," he said as he turned and stalked out of the room.

"Don't try to leave, they'll just bring you back to me," he said over his shoulder.

She shuffled over to a chair and sat, holding her hands out in front of her and frowning at the irritated skin on her wrists. Her attention on the pain, she didn't notice him squat in front of her, a jar in his hands. Hissing, she looked up as he smeared the white cream on her angry skin, the coolness taking out some of the burn.

"This should help," he commented as he scooped up more of the cream and smeared it on the burns on her neck. "Better?"

"Yeah," she whispered, watching as concern moved across his face, replacing the anger she'd noticed earlier. "Thank you, Asher," she said, calling him by the name she'd heard the slimy king guy use. He'd been surly to her before, why was he being so nice?

With a grimace he stated, "My real name is Brock. Brock Atkinson. I'm here on the orders of The Alpha to gather information about this pack and its leader." He made sure all of the burns were covered with the cream.

"Well then, thank you, Brock." She wondered what or who an Alpha was but she was too tired to care.

After wiping the excess cream off his fingers, he set the jar on the table. "How about some water?"

She frowned, not wanting to owe this man any more than she already did. "It's okay. I'll be fine," she said as she stood. "Thanks for getting me out of there, but I think I should leave now."

"I can't let you do that." He stood in front of her, putting his hands on her arms. "What is your name? Who is your pack?"

"What is so important about my pack?" she asked with a sigh. "That asshole kept asking me that too."

She shivered when he stared into her eyes. "Without a pack affiliation you're fair game."

"Fair game? What does that mean?"

"Any pack that needs females can basically force you to mate with whomever they choose."

Her eyes widened. "What?" she screeched.

"Without a pack you're considered a Rogue. It's an ancient rule but most packs still follow it." He led her back to the chair. "Sit."

He paced the length of the room and back muttering to himself, "How did she grow up outside a pack?" Back in front of her, he questioned her again. "Let's start with your name."

She sighed. "I go by Mac."

"Last name?"

"Smith."

"Seriously? Smith?"

"That's the name they gave me," she said, her arms crossed over her chest.

"Who gave you that name?"

"Child Protective Services." She looked out the window as she continued. "They think I was about six years old when I was found abandoned in a convenience store in Florida."

His eyes narrowed. "Abandoned?"

"Yeah," she sighed. "They told me I didn't talk for almost a year after I was found. My t-shirt had Mac written on the tag so I became Mac Smith."

She coughed, her throat dry. "Could I get that water now?"

"Sure," he said as he walked back to the kitchen, returning with a couple of bottles of water and a can of peanuts."

She took the water and refused the peanuts. "Allergic," she said simply.

He set the peanuts on the table. "That's…" he paused as if looking for the right word, "interesting."

"Will you let me go now?" she asked? "I'm good at disappearing."

"No," he said before picking up the peanuts and returning them to the kitchen.

"How are you going to stop me?" she asked as he walked back into the room.

"By being honest with you." He sat on the couch, put his elbows on his legs, and began his story. "When I was ten, we lived next door to the ruling family of the Red Tail Pack. They had three kids, a boy my age, a younger boy, and the youngest, a girl. That summer they went on vacation and were involved in a car accident in the mountains of Tennessee that killed the parents. The boys, Harley and Levi, survived but the girl disappeared. They theorized she wandered away and died out in the wilderness."

"What does that have to do with me? I was found in Florida?"

"Your eyes."

"What about my eyes?" she asked as she stared at him.

"That color of green is rare in a Were, I know of only one family with eyes that color. Tell me, what color is your Wolf?"

"What does the color of my wolf have to do with anything?"

"Just tell me, what color?"

"Red," she answered in a huff. "Don't know what is so important about the color of my wolf."

"It all fits," he mumbled. Pulling his phone out of his

pocket he dialed and waited. "Yeah, I've got news for The Alpha. I think I found McKayla."

Mac

Mac rolled onto her back and stared at the ceiling, counting the tiles as her mind whirled. She might have a family, brothers. A brother who was The Alpha, the head Alpha of all North American Weres, kinda like a king. She brushed at a tear that rolled down her cheek. Her one wish growing up was to have a family. Afraid to believe it to be true, she tried to sleep. Tossing and turning, she couldn't help but remember the terror she'd felt the first time her Wolf had made her presence known to her. She'd innocently told her foster parents about the voice in her head and they'd immediately returned her to Child Protective Services, like a defective appliance. The next couple of years had been a series of visits to a psychologist until she learned to tell them the voice was gone.

Labeled as having a mental illness, she ended up in a group home, running away when she turned sixteen after her Wolf told her it was time to go. That first change had her questioning whether she really was crazy. Scared and alone, her Wolf had helped her navigate the world and stay out of sight, living rough and stealing to keep herself fed.

Twice she'd been caught and returned to the group home and labeled as a troublemaker. The third time she ran away she ran north up into Georgia, finding a group of homeless in Atlanta that taught her how to live on the streets. The first time she'd smelled the otherness of Weres, she'd come upon them as they beat up a woman and stole her purse. She ran, terrified they'd steal what little she possessed. Avoiding all Weres, she'd traveled north up into Indiana, stopping outside

Fort Wayne for a run during the last full moon. She hadn't been as careful as normal, too excited by the prospect of running through the small forest. Then she awoke trussed up and lying on that cold, stone floor, wearing only her jeans and shirt.

Unable to fall asleep, she got up and padded to the door of the bedroom and opened it slowly before stepping out into the hall. Her only interactions with Weres hadn't been a pleasant experience so she tiptoed toward the front door.

"Where do you think you're going?"

She jumped at the voice behind her. Crap, he'd heard her. "Uh, I just need a drink of water," she fibbed as she turned to look at him.

"From where, the corner store? The kitchen is over there," he said as he motioned with his right hand, his left hand in his pocket as he leaned in the doorway.

"I don't trust you."

"That's obvious." He stepped toward her. "Don't you want to know if you have family? A family who has been searching for you for fourteen years."

She stared at him, jutting out her hip in attitude. "Well, yeah, but…"

He smirked. "Go back to bed, Mac. I need sleep. Getting you out of here now that you've captured the interest of Gladieaux will be difficult. I'm supposed to take you back to the throne room tomorrow with answers as to your name and pack. Obviously, I can't tell him what I suspect."

"Can't you lie? Tell him I'm nobody?"

"I have to be very careful, Gladieaux has a way of knowing if someone is lying. I've been able to keep my cover intact so far, but I won't be able to keep it up for long. I've got to figure out a way to get us both out of here that he will believe."

She looked down at her feet. "Just let me go. I don't want to cause you problems."

Brock's face went hard. "No," he growled as his wolf forced its way forward. "This is too important. Plus, what kind of friend would I be if I knew I found his sister and didn't do everything I could to return her to her family?"

"Fine, even though I'm not sure I believe this whole sister thing." she said with a sigh. Turning on her heel, she walked back to the bedroom, She had to admit, she was tired of scraping by, renting rooms in disgusting hotels that didn't care that she didn't have ID or a credit card. Dammit, she could take care of herself but the prospect of having siblings made her question her stance on accepting help from this guy. This Were who seemed to be a good guy as opposed to that other guy who was a complete asshole. Living on the fringe of society, she knew how things could be hidden from the general public, just under the surface where normal people didn't like to look. After shucking off her jeans and dropping them on the floor she stretched out on the bed and pulled the covers over herself, relishing the feel of the cool cotton against her skin.

It was barely dawn when Mac opened her eyes, the smell of coffee wafting through the open door. She snuck to the bathroom after donning her jeans, wishing she had her backpack. Running her fingers through her hair, she inspected the roots, frowning at the red hair showing, she much preferred the pink she'd dyed it a couple of weeks before.

After a quick shower, mainly to wash the dirt off her feet, she dressed in her dirty clothes. Using her finger and the toothpaste she found in the medicine cabinet she brushed her teeth so at least her mouth tasted clean. Running her hands down her shirt, she brushed at the dirty spots. Oh well, until she could talk this guy into going after her backpack it was all she had. At least her feet were clean, she didn't want to look at the sheets on the bed, they were probably filthy. A tap on the bathroom door had her spinning to look at it, as if she could see through it.

"You done in there? Breakfast is ready."

When she opened the door the smell of bacon wafted through, making her stomach grumble. She motioned to her clothes with her hands, "Until I can get my stuff, this is as good as it gets."

"The wolves who found you probably took it. We'll get you some things when we get out of here. If it's not today we can throw your stuff in the wash."

She smiled. "I doubt they found my backpack, I hid it pretty well. I never leave my backpack anywhere near where I leave my clothes when I go on a run."

He turned to the stove and scooped scrambled eggs out of the pan, filling the plate in his hand. "Sit, eat," he said as he set the plate of eggs on the table, next to a plate of bacon. "Toast will be up in a sec." He turned back to the stove and filled another plate with eggs.

Mac tried to eat slowly but the eggs were fluffy and tasted so good she started shoveling food in her mouth, hardly chewing before she swallowed.

"Hey, slow down. Nobody's going to take it away from you." He looked at her, concern on his face. "How long has it been since you've eaten?"

"Yesterday morning I found most of a breakfast sandwich in the trash," she mumbled as she stared down at the plate. She picked up a piece of bacon and broke it into pieces. "I was out of cash and I was going to hunt on my run but…"

"Jesus," he muttered. "I should have fed you last night. It was so late I didn't even think about it."

"It's okay, I'm used to skipping meals."

Chapter Three

Brock

He stared at the phone in his hand, willing it to ring. Harley had been skeptical about Mac's identity but Brock was sure it was McKayla. It was the eyes, and her resemblance to her family, especially their mom. Through the wariness he saw in them, he also saw the laughing green eyes he remembered. Emerald green to be exact, so brilliant they almost glowed against the creamy skin of her face. Now, the skin was darker, tanned from her time spent living rough and walking to get wherever she needed to go. Her story of odd jobs done for cash made him want to hit something, preferably whoever it was that took her from that accident scene and then abandoned her months later in another state. Now, she was on the radar of Gladiaux. Hopefully he could get her out of town before her real identity was discovered. No way they'd be able to leave if they knew she was sister to Harley Jensen, The Alpha over all the pack alphas. To him he was just Harley, his best friend. After the accident Harley and Levi had been inconsolable, having lost most of their family. Brock's parents had taken in the orphaned brothers, keeping up the search for their sister until all leads had been followed. Over the years there'd been no trace of her found. Brock's dad had been the Red Tail Pack's Beta so he'd stepped up to take over until Harley was of age to become The Alpha. Unlike regular pack Alphas who could be challenged by anyone who coveted the position, Weres had to be of a certain lineage to challenge The Alpha.

When his phone rang, Brock took a deep breath and accepted the call.

"Brock, man, you sure?" Harley asked, forgoing any form of greeting, continuing their conversation from the previous evening as if it hadn't been seven hours previous.

"Yeah, it's the eyes, and the hair. Plus, she looks just like your mom." Brock held his breath and waited for his friend's response.

"Shit, brother…" Harley started but stopped.

"I know. When I first saw her eyes it hit me, the resemblance is uncanny." He paced the bedroom. "Problem is getting her out of here without Gladiaux figuring out who she is or who I'm working for. I could use some help here, brother."

"Mitch is on his way to you. We've got a plan."

"Hope he gets here soon; things are getting out of hand. Gladiaux is an ass and I'm ready to take him down."

"You know we can't do that yet; we don't have the proof to back up our claims. Let's get you out of there and we'll make a new plan."

With a growl Brock's wolf muttered, *Someone's here*. He heard a knock on his front door. "Gotta go. My Wolf doesn't like whoever's at the door." He hit end, not waiting for a response from his friend.

He pulled open the bedroom door to find Mac pressed up

against the wall in the hallway. "Quick, in the closet," he prompted as grabbed a bottle off the dresser. If we have to run, spray this all over yourself. I know it stinks but it'll cover up your scent."

Slipping his cover persona into place, he walked to the front door, picking up his sunglasses from the table and slipping them on.

Gladiaux's Beta, Tony, stood on his porch, his face expressionless. "Boss wants to see you now. And bring the girl with you."

"Gotcha," he murmured. "She's a feisty one," he said with a grin, his stomach rolling.

The Beta grinned. "If you get tired of her," he said as he winked.

Stomach churning, Brock slammed the door before stomping to the bedroom. "Change of plans," he said as he opened the door. "We have to go to Gladiaux right now."

Her eyes widened, "What does he want?" she asked as she slipped the bottle into her pocket.

"I don't know and that worries me." He picked up his jacket from the bed. "Here, put this on."

Pulling her behind him, he hurried back to Gladiaux's throne room. "I need you to act like you've submitted to my Wolf."

She stiffened, "I submit to no one," she cried as his grip on her wrist tightened.

"Get over it. If he suspects you haven't submitted, he'll know something isn't right. I've spent months cultivating his trust and I won't have you screwing that up. We only need to get through this and then we'll go to your brother."

He watched as she realized he was right. "Okay, let's get this over with."

"Eyes down and act submissive," he hissed at her as the door opened in front of him.

Walking through the door into the throne room, Brock scanned the crowd that had gathered. Gathered. *Shit, what the hell is Gladiaux up to?*

Mac shivered, her eyes going wide at the crowd before she remembered to stare at the floor.

Brock tapped her wrist slightly with his index finger to remind her of their plan. Pulling her behind him, he strode to the middle of the room directly in front of the throne where Gladieux slouched.

"Well? Did you get any answers out of her? Her pack?"

Thankful for the mirrored lenses on his sunglasses, he said, "She's from the White Paw Pack in the upper peninsula of Michigan. She was only thirteen when she ran off, too young to have been through a Fealty ceremony, so no tattoo."

Gladiaux sneered, "White Paw? No wonder she doesn't have any manners." He picked at a fingernail before continuing. "I guess it doesn't matter now, she'll be a part of the Black Paw Pack once you pledge fealty to me. I'm feeling generous, I'll give you time to get her outfitted in appropriate clothing for a fealty celebration." He waved his hand, "Tonight will be soon enough. Be prepared to take part in the ceremony, we'll go ahead and have the mating ceremony too."

Brock smiled. "Looking forward to it." He turned and calmly walked out of the room.

"No way I'm taking part in a mating ceremony," Mac muttered, loud enough that one of the Weres guarding the door heard it.

He laughed as he explained, "She's still learning manners. Don't worry, she'll act appropriately tonight at the ceremony."

"You'd better hope so," the guard replied as he stepped out of Brock's way.

"Hurry up, Mac, we have some shopping to do."

Mac

Mac stood in front of the mirror and brushed her hair, wishing they had time for her to dye it again. The red roots really bothered her for some reason. The dress Brock had picked was nothing like what she would have picked for herself though she had to admit she looked good in it. A short dress in white that showed off the tan of her skin with a tied belt that accentuated her waist. It was shorter than she liked but if Brock thought it was appropriate... She wished she didn't feel so pretty, the thought of participating in any cere-mony had her nervous as hell. What happened at a fealty ceremony anyway?

Brock tapped on the doorframe to get her attention. When she turned around she watched his jaw go hard. *What, was the dress unacceptable?*

"Fuck," he muttered as he handed her the shoes in his hand.

She ran her hands down the skirt of her dress. "Do I look okay?" Her Wolf fidgeted with nerves as she waited for his answer.

"You look... nice."

Had his eyes flashed when he said nice? She knew she looked good but he was frowning at her like she was wearing her dress backwards or something.

"I'll meet you out front," he ground out before he disap-peared down the hallway.

She turned back to the mirror and took once last look,

wondering what about the dress had Brock in such a strange mood.

Sitting on the bed, she strapped on the shoes, thankful he'd let her pick out something low heeled. She'd practically drooled over a pair of sky-high heels but she knew those would be a mistake if they had to make a run for it. Besides, she'd never worn anything other than trainers or flats. Stepping toward the bedroom door, she was doubly thankful she hadn't given into the call of the sexy heels, she didn't feel quite steady on even these low heels, the high ones would have been impossible for her to walk in comfortably.

She sauntered out the front door, closing it softly behind her, noticing how Brock's gaze followed her. Her Wolf preened, she knew she looked good.

"It's about time. You ready?" Brock practically growled at her.

Geez, what crawled up his ass?

As they walked down the street toward the square, Brock started to explain about the Fealty celebration. "Now, the Fealty celebration is normally a yearly ceremony where all the Weres of the pack pledge their allegiance to the current Alpha. There was one a couple of months ago so I don't know why Gladieux is having another so soon. He'll be expecting me to pledge my fealty to him but I can't do that, it's already pledged to your brother, The Alpha."

"Why do you keep calling my brother The Alpha instead of his name?"

"I'll explain later. Right now, remember to act submissive to me." He pulled her along behind him.

"Will I be expected to make this pledge? Do I even have a choice?"

Brock sighed and ran his left hand through his hair. "He'll

expect you to make the pledge since you don't have a pack tattoo. But don't worry, I'll figure out a way to keep that from happening."

Chapter Four

Brock

When Mac turned around and he'd seen her in the dress, his Wolf had growled, *Mine*. Accentuating her curves, the dress had her adequately covered but it somehow enhanced her beauty, the short skirt showing off her toned legs. He wanted nothing more than to pull her to the bed and claim her as his. Panting, his wolf strained to be let out, to claim his mate. *Not now!*

"Sooon," his Wolf cried loud enough that he was worried Mac would hear.

He handed her the shoes and hightailed it out of the room before he gave in to his Wolf.

As his Wolf paced, Brock stepped into the shower, letting the hot water beat against the back of his neck, hoping it would relieve some of the tension that had settled there. His thoughts turned to Mac and how he wanted to get lost in those green eyes. He let himself imagine her wet body pressed up against his, her hand reaching between them and taking hold of his cock.

He let the imagined encounter play out in his mind as he stroked himself, imagining it was her hand. Balls drawing up tight and his breath locked in his lungs he stroked faster until his body let go with a rush of warmth and the feeling of a tightly wound spring releasing.

Letting the water cleanse away the evidence of his orgasm, he resigned himself to more self-satisfaction until he could find a willing female, he couldn't take advantage of Mac's sexual inexperience. She was his best friend's little sister. He could practically smell her virginity and it was driving his Wolf berserk.

Brock pulled Mac into the auditorium behind him, the scent of Were's mating heavy in the air. Shit, he'd hoped to arrive after the mating ceremony was completed. Only the mating bite was required, but obviously this pack went further, with full on consummation. In most packs the actual consummation was done later, in private. Gladieux had specifically mentioned the Mating Ceremony, so he was going to have to figure something out. Maybe he could convince his Wolf to only bite hard enough to draw a little blood, make it look like he'd actually taken her as a mate.

The smell of female arousal wafted through the air, making his Wolf growl and strain at the hold Brock had on him. "*Mate*," his Wolf growled".

"*We can't touch her, she's the sister of The Alpha,*" Brock was determined to deliver Mac to The Alpha untouched.

Mac watched the couple completing their mating consummation in the center of the room, the Wolves around howling as the scent of sex wound them all up.

Gladieux stepped off the dais and sauntered to Brock. "As you can see, I brought back public consummation. I think it's much more meaningful this way."

Brock held his expression, fighting the urge to sneer at

this pompous asshole. "Yeah, haven't heard of any packs still doing it this way."

"I'm glad you approve, you and that little female are next."

Brock balled his hand into a fist and fought to keep from punching him. Crap, he should have explained to Mac how this worked.

"My female is feeling a bit edgy with all the Wolves here. May I take her out of the room and calm her down first?"

"I suppose but be quick about it. This crowd could get unruly fast so we don't want to keep them waiting." With a laugh he motioned to a door to the left of the dais. "Use my personal office."

He felt Mac pull against the grip he had on her wrist and gasp at the pain. "Come on, Little One, let's go get you calmed down."

When the door shut behind them Brock blew out a breath and turned to look at Mac. The terrified look in her eyes tore at his heart.

"Don't worry, we won't be 'fornicating' in public." He paced the length of the room and back, stopping in front of Mac. We just need for them to believe we will. I'll figure out a way to stop the ceremony before that point."

Mac looked at him dubiously. "How will you..." Her question was cut off by a sharp knocking on the door.

He opened the door to find one of Gladieux's Wolves standing on the porch.

"They're ready for you. I suggest you don't keep Alpha Gladieux waiting."

"Trust me," Brock said to Mac as he took her hand in his. "And look like the thought of this doesn't completely terrify you."

"I'll try."

He squeezed her hand and ushered her out the door.

They returned to the ceremony where all eyes in the room were trained on them. Brock frantically tried to come up with a plan.

Jase motioned Brock and Mac forward to stand in front of the dais where Gladieux was ensconced on his throne. With a slight bow, he stepped back.

Gladieux stood and pointed at the couple. "Asher, do you take this female as your mate?"

Brock stood tall and answered loudly so everyone could here, "Yes, I take this female as my mate." His throat locked up and he swallowed hard so he could recite the next part of the traditional vow. "For the rest of my days."

The crowd clapped, happy to have another mating to watch.

Gladieux turned his attention to Mac. "And you? Do you take Asher to be your mate for the rest of your days?"

Mac looked up at Brock, her eyes searching his. At his slight nod she said quietly, "Yes, I do."

Brock inhaled and frantically tried to find a way out of this mess. The biting part of the ceremony was quick and he had to find a way to stop the ceremony before their actual consummation.

Brock pulled off his clothes as his wolf came forward and his body changed. *"Mine"* his Wolf growled as he stepped toward Mac.

Mac

Eyes wide, she watched as Brock morphed into a wolf, his blue eyes peering out from the animal's face. Was that how it looked when she changed? She'd never seen another were change into their Wolf form before.

After a deep breath she reminded herself this wasn't real, it was just a show so they could get away from this pack. Brock had reassured her that this would not be binding.

She turned her back to Brock's Wolf and shrugged off the jacket before pulling her hair toward her right shoulder blade and out of the way. She felt the hot breath of Brock's Wolf just before the pain of his bite into her left shoulder. With a wince she almost dropped his jacket as she felt a burning– the beginnings of the magical tattoo that would become permanent when their bonding was consummated fully.

She turned around and watched as Brock morphed back into his human form. She practically drooled over the muscles of his arms and chest and then she looked lower and almost gasped at the sight of his penis, standing out strait from his body.

Brock grabbed her shoulders and pulled her to him, dropping his mouth to hers and kissed her until she looked up at him in a daze.

"Well, that's not the normal next step but whatever works for you I guess," Gladieux said with a laugh. "Now, for the final step – consummation."

The double doors slammed as one of the outside guards hurried up to the dais.

With a bow he looked up at Gladieux with a frown.

"Why have you interrupted the ceremony?"

The guard looked at the floor and mumbled, "I'm sorry for the interruption but there's someone here to see you."

"Why would you bust in here for that? Go tell them to wait, I'll see them after the ceremony is completed."

"Bur, Alpha, it's the Grey Moon Pack Alpha, Colin Hayward."

"Shit," Gladieux muttered. "Escort him to my office through the back door and I'll be there momentarily."

The guard turned and hurried out of the room.

Speaking louder Gladieux addressed the crowd, "I'm sorry, but the rest of the ceremony will have to wait. An important matter needs my attention immediately." He strode to his office door and slammed it behind him.

Brock let out a breath and silently gave thanks to whoever it was that showed up.

And then Mac blew their chance to get away clean by asking in a low whisper, "Does that mean we can leave, Brock?"

The guard standing about five feet away turned and stared at them.

"Stop," he growled, "why did she call you Brock?"

"Shit," Brock said as he pulled Mac in closer to him. "Get behind me."

The Were at the door pulled out a knife and swiped it at Brock.

"I didn't want it to go this way," Brock muttered as he pulled the gun out of the back of his jeans. Aiming at the guard, he pulled the trigger as he grabbed Mac's wrist again.

"Run," he yelled, he pushing her through the door ahead of him. Bullets whizzed around them as they ran across the square. "Head for your backpack, I'll find you there."

He let go of her and she watched as he let out his Wolf mid-stride, four paws hitting the ground. With a growl he turned and snarled.

The other guard stopped and stared, changing into wolf form on the fly like that was difficult if not impossible. Armed with a gun instead of a knife he aimed and took a shot.

Brock's front leg crumpled underneath him and he hit the

29

ground. Lurching to his feet he limped to the cover provided by the houses that lined this side of the square.

She kicked off the useless heeled shoes and took off running toward the edge of town, not looking back. Shots rang out and she ducked as she heard the bullets whiz past her, kicking up puffs of dirt around her feet. Forcing herself to keep running, she zigzagged around houses, trying to confuse any pursuers until she reached the forest and the extra cover of the underbrush. Once she reached her backpack, she stopped long enough to pull on Brock's jacket and then settle her backpack onto her shoulders as she scanned the forest for a hiding place to wait for Brock to find her. A fallen tree over a ditch created a small hidden spot where she could rest and watch for anyone following her. Pulling Brock's jacket tighter around her she leaned back and watched, her eyelids drooping as her sleepless night caught up with her.

A branch behind her snapped and woke her from her uneasy slumber. She'd been in the middle of a nightmare of crumpled metal and burning rubber. Breathing in slowly to dispel the imagined smell she held her breath when another branch snapped.

"Jesus, Brock, where the fuck are you?" the man muttered, his eyes watching the ground in front of him. He stopped and looked closer at something on the forest floor. He stood up and sniffed the air. "It's okay. I won't hurt you."

Terrified of being found, Mac held herself still, hoping this guy would just move along.

"Have you seen a guy wearing mirrored shades?" He waited, his eyes still scanning the forest. "I know you're there, I can smell you."

"Who's your pack?" she asked, hoping he didn't say Black Paw.

He stood straighter and said, "Red Paw. Are you Mac?"

She crawled out of her hiding spot. Standing, she brushed at the dirt on her dress as she turned to face him. "Who are you? Where's Brock?"

"Brock isn't with you? He asked. "What happened?"

"I blew his cover," she said with a sob. "He told me to run and he turned to face them. I heard shots. I didn't mean to do it, his name just slipped out."

"Shit, that doesn't sound good."

A rustle in the ground cover to the east had them both standing still and listening. "What was that?" she asked in a whisper.

"Get back in your hiding spot," he replied as he crouched down below the top of the undergrowth.

A wolf limped into view, bleeding from its shoulder.

The strange man stood, "Brock!"

Mac crawled out of her hiding spot at his shout. She stopped and stared as the wolf changed back into its human form. Brock crumpled to the ground, blood running down from a hole in his shoulder.

The man knelt next to him, rummaging in his pack. "What happened?"

"Bullet...coated...wolfsbane." Brock said each word between a pant.

"Son of a bitch," he muttered as he pulled a first-aid kit out of his pack. "Gotta get that bullet out." A syringe full of a clear liquid in his hand, he prepared to inject it into Brock's arm.

"No." Brock growled, "No pain killers. Just do it. Can't be out, we gotta move fast," he mumbled.

"You sure?"

"Yeah, just do it already. I can feel it in there, the burning is spreading."

Mac knelt at Brock's back and put her hand on his shoulder. "Lean back into me." She handed him a stick about the thickness of one of his fingers. "Here, bite this." She hoped this would help, that's what they always did in those old westerns.

Taking the stick, he put it in his mouth and leaned into her.

Heat radiated off him, as if he was burning from the inside out. Mac placed her hand on the side of his face. "God, Brock, you're burning up." She looked up at the stranger. "Hurry up!"

"Hold him still," the man said with a frown. "This is gonna hurt like a bitch." He pressed the tip of the forceps in his hand into the wound, feeling around for the bullet.

Brock grunted and went slack against her when the man muttered, "Got it," He pulled the forceps out of the wound, dropping the bullet covered in the red of Brock's blood onto a medical sponge. Blood seeped out of the wound and he pressed a fresh sponge against it.

Brock moaned, his eyelids fluttering as he fought to regain consciousness.

Mac brushed at the hair on Brock's forehead, the heat from his fevered skin seeping into her fingers.

Brock's eyelids fluttered and he tried to sit up. "We gotta…"

"Shhh… take a minute, big guy."

"Mac? You okay?"

"Me, I'm great, you, not so much."

"Is she okay. Mitch?" he asked as if he didn't believe her answer.

"Yeah, she's good." He replied before turning his attention to Mac, "I'm Mitch, The Alpha sent me to help Mitch get you back to Fort Wayne."

Brock sat up and gingerly rotated his arm, wincing at the pain. "It'll do. We've got to move. Gladieux's men have to be searching for us." His eyes glazed from pain he continued, "We need to get some real estate between us and them." He scanned the small clearing. "How far are we from town?"

The man placed a pad on the wound in Brock's shoulder and started wrapping gauze around him to hold it in place.

"Only a couple of miles. We've got to get you patched up before we do anything else." After tying off the end of the gauze Mitch unbuttoned his shirt and took it off. "Here," he said as he handed it to Brock, "this will have to do until we can get to my truck. It will at least help keep the bandage clean."

Brock winced as he moved his arm to put on the shirt.

Mitch closed his eyes and shook his head, "Won't even take a minute to recover. You're still a stubborn son of a bitch." He packed up the first aid kit. "My truck is close. Once we get far enough away from this backwards town we can shift and let your wolf speed up your healing." He put Brock's uninjured arm across his shoulders and started toward his truck. "Come on, Mac, we've got to move!"

She trotted behind the two men, constantly looking back over her shoulder for any sign of pursuit. With an oof she ran into the back of Brock, her shoulder hitting the back of his.

Brock groaned and the man shushed him, "Quiet, I heard something." He stopped and sniffed the air. "Shit, they've found my truck."

Brock sagged against him.

"Dammit, Brock, you've got to move, buddy."

Mac shoved her hands in her pockets to keep them from shaking. How in the hell were they going to get away? Her left hand bumped into the bottle Brock had given her that morning.

"Will this help? Brock said it will help mask our scent. I think it stinks."

He opened the bottle and sniffed, "Oh geez, that is nasty but it might help. I wish there was more of it. This small amount shared between the three of us won't cover our scents for long."

He cocked his head and he sniffed the air again. "They're getting closer. We need to find somewhere to hide."

No hide, fight, her Wolf chanted in her head. *Go back for pup.*

Not now, she thought back, *but soon.*

The man ushered her to a downed tree, telling her to crawl over it and hide behind it. "Spray yourself and Brock, I'll lead them away." He handed her his keys "Maybe I'll get them far enough away that you can get to my truck.

"But how will you get away."

"Don't worry about me, I'll be fine." He pulled a card out of his wallet and wrote an address on the back. "Get to Fort Wayne and take him to this address, they'll be able to help him."

"But…"

"Just do it," He hissed as the snapping of twigs grew louder. He practically threw Mac over the downed tree before carefully hauling Brock over it. "Stay down until you're sure they're gone."

She held her breath and listened as he took off away from them. Dousing them both with the smelly concoction, she hoped it would work.

Huddling behind the log, her arms around Brock to keep him up against her, she closed her eyes and let the quiet of the forest wash over her. So many thoughts whirled through her mind. If Brock was right, she wasn't alone in the world, she had a family, brothers, and a pack. And she was free.

She hugged him tighter when he moaned, trying to quiet him in case Gladieux's men were still around. No way was she going back to Ankton to be led around on a leash. She was free and intended to stay that way.

Chapter Five

Mac held still, barely breathing, as the searchers wandered back and forth in the clearing, mere inches from their hiding place behind the fallen tree. It seemed Brock's smelly stuff worked really well at hiding their scents. The pungent aroma made her eyes water and her nose run but she didn't dare wipe at them or sniff.

The footsteps gradually receded back in the direction of town. Once she was sure they were gone she peeked over the dead tree, relieved to see the clearing was devoid of Weres. She roused Brock from an uneasy slumber and forced him up, draping his uninjured arm over her shoulders and slowly plodded in the direction of Mitch's truck. She'd never driven but surely it couldn't be that hard.

Brock's feet dragged along the ground, barely lifting enough to take a step. "Come on big guy, I need your help here."

She finally got him up near the truck and she realized she didn't have to worry about driving. Gladieux's men had taken no chances and slashed all four tires. Even she knew this truck wasn't going anywhere anytime soon.

"Shitballs," she muttered as Brock slid to the ground, his legs giving out completely. Bending over him she placed her hand against his forehead wincing at the heat radiating from him. Surely that wasn't good. "Dammit Brock, what am I supposed to do now?"

I smell water, her wolf commented as she sniffed the air again. *Not far.*

"That's just great. How am I supposed to get this big lug there? No way can I carry him." She sank to sit next to him and tried to pull some the heat out of his skin with her cool hands.

The keys in her pocket dug into her leg. *Maybe there's something in the truck that will help.*

Brock groaned when she stood, mumbling about green eyes and lost pups.

The bed of the truck was empty but she found camping equipment packed into the back seat. She was overjoyed to find a sleeping bag and a backpack containing a change of clothes and another first aid kit. At least she could change the bandage on his wound.

Pulling her pack off her back and pulling out what was now her only pair of jeans and one of her last two shirts. Fuckers, leaving her with almost nothing again.

She struggled to get the zipper of the dress pulled down, wincing at the pain of the bite mark on her left shoulder. The fabric sliding down her right shoulder blade made her hiss in pain as it dragged across the newly formed tattoo. She thought Brock had told her the tattoo wouldn't appear as he wasn't going to bite down hard enough to trigger the mating spell. He must have been wrong.

Oh well, *I'll worry about that later*, she thought as she pulled on her clothes. At least she had better freedom of movement. Hating to throw away the beautiful dress, she stuffed it in her pack and turned toward the backpack she'd pulled out of the truck. A metal mess kit clanked as she dropped it to the ground. She pulled out some freeze-dried food packets and other camping essentials. At the bottom she was overjoyed to discover a lightweight shiny silver blanket. At least she could cover Brock and try to keep him warm once the sun went down and the temperature dropped.

Unfortunately, she didn't find anything that would help her move the large man so she needed to find a sheltered spot for them to camp for the night unless Mitch happened to come back before nightfall. The sun dropped lower in the sky, heralding the onset of dusk and dashing her hopes of Mitch returning in time to help before night fell.

She dragged Brock back toward the fallen tree as she scanned the landscape for a better spot. As she pushed him over the fallen tree she noticed another fallen tree farther down the dried-up creek bed that looked like there was larger space underneath the one end. After a short climb she was at the other tree, pleased to discover a hollowed out space under the roots that looked to be above where the water would flow if it rained. She scanned the sky for clouds, hoping any rain would hold off until the next day. She sat for a moment and contemplated their situation. Should she use the space under the log or try to find something better? A cool breeze swept her hair off the back of her neck, making her shiver at the chill. She better get Brock moved and covered before the temperature dropped any further.

Fireflies flitted back and forth in the growing dusk as she pulled Brock up the creek bed, having to stop and rest way too often for her liking. Why did he have to be such a big guy? Once she had him in the space, she made sure to cover him with the blanket. After a quick trip downstream to look for dry wood, she returned to Brock's side and laid the wood next to him. Piling the wood into a slight depression in the ground, she used the lighter from her backpack to light a small bunch of twigs at the bottom. Once the flames were licking greedily at the larger branches pulled the edge of the blanket over herself and snuggled into Brock's warmth.

She opened her eyes and sighed at the touch of a warm hand at the side of her face. Her sleep hadn't been long, the fire still burned brightly, shadows leaping and falling as the flames consumed the wood. Curled into the body beside her, she shivered when he nipped at her earlobe.

Another delicious shiver ran down her body as Brock's lips found hers and his arm pulled her tighter to him. His tongue invaded her mouth and dueled with hers as his hands snuck under her shirt and splayed against her skin just above the waistband of her jeans. One hand moved down and unsnapped her pants as the other slid up and cupped her breast. She sighed as his fingers found the waistband of her underwear and dipped lower. She knew she should stop him, his skin still burned with the effects of the wolfsbane coursing through his veins. His hands pushed her shirt up and she pulled it off, a yearning she'd never felt before shoving her thoughts away. His mouth found the side of her neck and left a trail of open-mouthed kisses down her chest until his mouth found one breast and his tongue played with her nipple, the sensation zipping down to her core.

Rubbing against him did nothing to assuage the ache. And then his fingers found her clit and her whole body convulsed as he stroked and rubbed, until his fingers slipped inside her. The high of the orgasm waned and then his hand was gone and his cock was nudging at her opening. Just the thought of him inside her had her panting, another orgasm building quickly. Even in his delirium he knew they couldn't be heard. His mouth covered hers as he entered her and the second, even more intense orgasm ripped through her and she screamed. Muffled by his mouth over hers, her scream was undetectable from the night sounds of the woods around them.

She woke to the stinging pain of the magical mating tattoo embedding itself into the skin of her right shoulder blade.

Oh shit, what had they done? Maybe there was a way to undue the mating.

She'd have to figure it out later. The sun was peeking over the horizon and she needed to get them somewhere safer. The Wolves were sure to come back and continue their search.

Brock

Brock woke, surprised at the ache in his shoulder. Oh yeah, the bullet and the wolfsbane. Then, the stinging pain on his other shoulder blade. He remembered that feeling from his first fealty ceremony. He knew what that pain meant. His hazy fever dreams must have been more than dreams. His Wolf chuffed at him, he could feel the bastard grinning at him.

Fuck. He was so screwed. No way would Harley forgive him for this.

With a sigh he put his hand on Mac's arm to wake her, loving the feel of her backside up against his front. He sniffed at her hair and grimaced at the slight smell of the spray he'd given her to mask her scent. At least he now knew the stuff worked.

She stirred and pressed her butt up against his groin and his Wolf came forward, growling with lust. *Nope, no time for that now. We're already gonna be in deep shit for last night.*

With a sigh, his Wolf retreated and he touched Mac's arm again. "Mac? Time to wake up."

Mac yawned and stretched. He could feel when she realized she was leaning up against him as she tensed and jumped up.

"Oh, sorry, I guess I…" She picked up her clothes and put them on, horrified that she'd fallen asleep against him.

"It's okay."

She peered at him and reached out to feel his forehead. "Feels like your fever is finally gone."

"Yeah. wolfsbane usually isn't fatal but it does take a while to work its way through your system." He looked around, expecting to find Mitch across the smoldering ashes of a fire. "Where's Mitch. He wasn't part of my fever-dream was he?"

"Oh, is that his name? You didn't dream him. After he dug the bullet out of you, he led the Wolves away from us."

Brock reached into his pocket, relieved to find his phone. Swiping at the screen, he punched in his code and scrolled through the notifications, swearing when the screen went blank. "Dammit! How far are we from the truck? Did you find the truck?"

"Not far, but it's not going anywhere – they slashed all four tires."

He rubbed his hand over his face, wishing for a shower as the smell of the spray wafted to his nose. "I wonder what else they did to the truck. Hopefully the battery isn't dead so I can charge my phone."

"The light came on when I opened the door to get the camping gear last night."

He stood and stretched, thankful the weakness from the wolfsbane was gone. "I'll go scout around a little, make sure

Gladieux's men aren't anywhere around before we head to the truck. Stay here and out of sight."

Her stomach let out a loud rumble. "Look for some water, we both need to eat something."

Shifting to Wolf form, he bounded out of sight toward the truck.

Chapter Six

Mac

As soon as Brock was out of sight, Mac put her head in her hands. He hadn't mentioned anything about the mating tattoo so maybe it had been her imagination. She stood and began gathering more wood to rekindle the fire. Surely they would have time to rehydrate some food and make coffee. She had a good-sized pile of sticks gathered when she heard the snap of a twig.

Whirling around she saw Brock's Wolf as he morphed back into his human form. The play of light and shadow on his muscles had her face feeling hot and her Wolf pacing. "*Mate,*" her Wolf whined.

"Oh, shut up about that already. We can't keep him," she muttered testily.

"No sign of Mitch," Brock commented as he donned his jeans.

Mac was almost sorry to see him get dressed. Surely just one more time... She shook her head to dispel thoughts about what they'd done the night before.

"I sure hope he didn't get picked up by Gladieux's men." He rummaged in the backpack and pulled out the clean t-shirt. "There's a stream just down the way if you want to wash up. If we go together, one of us can stand watch while the other cleans up."

"Getting this stink off of me would be amazing." She grabbed her pack and stood, waiting for him to lead the way. "Oh wait," she said as she looked around her little campsite, practically pouncing on the mess kit. "There's coffee and some freeze-dried food. Do you think we have time?" she asked as she stuffed it into her pack.

"Let's get cleaned up first and then we'll see."

Well, that was better than a "no', so she plodded along behind him, enjoying watching the muscles in his back as he hadn't put on the clean shirt.

Ten minutes later and she was watching as Brock stood in the middle of the creek, the water coming up just over his knees. A noise had her attention back to the open area to the west, watching out for any sign of Mitch or Gladieux's men. Her thoughts and her gaze drifted back to the man standing naked and splashing water on himself.

Shaking her head to dispel the erotic thoughts, she saw movement at the edge of the clearing. Her Wolf whined as she stood.

A lone form stepped out from the trees and she watched as they scanned the clearing.

Her Wolf sniffed and she felt her smile. "*Friend.*" She stood and watched him move closer. She wanted to stand and wave since her Wolf was satisfied but who knew who else might see or hear her.

Mitch trotted up to her. "Where's Brock?" he asked worriedly.

She pointed over her shoulder. "He's fine. Just washing

off the stink. Please tell me you didn't see anyone near here, it's my turn next."

With a grin he said. "No, haven't seen any of Gladieux's men today."

Brock climbed the bank and smiled at Mitch. "Glad to see you weren't captured."

"What, you know me better than that. You think those yahoos could capture me?"

Brock clapped him on the shoulder. "Sorry about your truck."

Mitch winced. "At least it's just flat tires, they could have done a lot worse."

"Okay, my turn," Mac said as she skipped down the bank, pulling off her shirt as she neared the creek.

The cool water felt good against her skin. She rubbed the water over where she'd applied the stinky spray and was delighted to discover that just the water got rid of the smell. Happily splashing in the water, she didn't see Brock frowning at Mitch.

"Eyes off," he growled, as his Wolf tried to come forward.

Mitch put his hands up as he took one last peek at Mac's naked back. "Oh, so that's how it is. That didn't take long."

"I know she should be off limits, especially as she's probably Harley's sister. Just the thought of asking him for permission…" his voice trailed off as he watched Mac bend over to scrub at her legs. "Argh… just kill me now," he muttered.

Mitch grinned. "Good to know that the Iceman can be melted," referencing the nickname Brock had picked up with his ability to keep his emotions locked down and out of sight no matter the situation.

Mitch took another look at Mac and frowned. "Is that what I think it is?"

With a scowl Brock turned away from his friend. "I thought it was a fever-dream brought on by the wolfsbane until I felt the tattoo forming. How the fuck am I supposed to explain to Harley and Levi that I am mated to their long lost sister? They're both going to freak out."

Movement at the tree line across the meadow caught Mitch's attention. "If we don't move now, you may never get the chance to find out."

With a scowl, Brock looked to verify that someone was there. "Fuck, it looks like at least five of them. If it was just one, I'd take care of him but that many raises the risk of something going wrong." He turned back to look at Mac who was starting to pull on her jeans. His wolf whined as he watched her creamy skin disappear beneath the cotton of her t-shirt. "Mac, hurry up, we've got company."

She turned and looked at him, her face determined as she picked up her dirty shirt and stuffed it into her pack. "Let's go."

Mitch pulled out his phone and frowned at the screen. "Still no fucking bars. Worthless piece of shit," he muttered as he shoved it back in his pocket. "We need backup."

"Can't worry about that now. We need to move before they catch up with us." Brock said as he picked up his shirt. "Let's go."

"Once we get far enough away, we can switch to Wolf form and make better time. I don't want to leave anything they can use to track us."

Chapter Seven

Mac

She stared out the window at the corn fields rushing past. It felt like they'd been running from Gladieux's men for weeks but it had only been a few days. She'd nearly wept with relief when The Alpha's men had shown up. Gladieux's men had backed off when they caught sight of the men wearing jackets emblazoned with the crest of the Red Tail Pack.

Brock had held her close when the men all stared at her, wondering if she was the girl they'd been searching for for almost fifteen years. They whispered among themselves, making Mac feel self-conscious about the dirty clothes she was wearing.

The SUV they were in stopped in front of a large house, the kind of house Mac had dreamt about living in for as long as she could remember. The door opened and two red-haired men stepped out into the sun. She didn't recognize them but they felt... familiar.

"Is that?" she asked Brock.

"The one on the left is Harley, The Alpha, and the other is Levi. He's The Beta."

"They look mad," she muttered as she squeezed closer to Brock.

"They're not mad, they're just... intense." Brock stepped out of the vehicle and turned back to her. "Don't be scared." He held his hand out to her.

Knowing there was no way to get out of this meeting she took his hand and stepped out of the car, wishing they'd stopped so she could have at least washed her hair.

Harley stepped toward them and stopped, his eyes going wide as he gazed at her face. "Fuck, McKayla? It really is you."

Before she could answer she was in his arms as he hugged her. She thought being hugged would feel like being a prisoner but it didn't. It felt right. She looked up at his face and saw a lone tear drip off his cheekbone.

"Our pack has been searching for you since the accident. Fifteen years we've been searching."

"My turn," Levi said roughly as he stood next to his brother and watched as his sister was welcomed back to their pack. Shifting from foot to foot he waited until Harley released her. "My God, I've waited so long for this day." Another long hug and Levi set her away from him and peered at her face. "You're right, Brock, she looks just like Mom."

Harley stepped toward the crowd that had gathered as news of McKayla's return had spread through the pack.

"We owe a huge debt to Brock Atkinson for returning our lost member to us. We need time to reacquaint her to our pack. There will be a celebration tomorrow."

Harley put his arm over Mac's shoulders and steered her toward the door of the house.

Brock

He stared after them as they entered the house, knowing he must tell his Alpha what transpired. That Mac (he still couldn't think of her as McKayla – she was his Mac) was his mate. Levi turned back.

"Brock? You coming?"

"Yeah, sure," he muttered as he forced his feet to carry him into the house. The tight rein he had on his emotions almost snapped when the door closed behind him. His best friends were going to see this as a betrayal, or at least a breach of Wolf etiquette. With a sigh he followed the group into the kitchen where a pot of spaghetti sauce simmered on the stove next to a pot ready for the pasta. He wished for the time to go home and shower, and some fresh clothes would have been awesome but when your Alpha tells you to be there, you be there.

He walked up behind Mac as she stared at the wall of pictures. When she reached up to touch the last picture of their whole family he had to fight back a growl. They, no he, had to find the person responsible for her abduction from the accident scene. He had to know why. Agitated, his Wolf paced as he thought about the day he'd heard about the accident and her disappearance.

He'd wondered why all the Wolves of the pack were snarling at each other. His father looked sad when he'd taken him into the house and sat him on the couch.

"What's wrong, Dad? Everyone is so… grouchy."

"The Jensens were in an accident today. Harley and Levi are okay but their parents…" His voice cracked as he continued, "didn't make it."

The sadness on his dad's face made Brock want to cry.

Then he realized his dad hadn't mentioned McKayla. "You said Harley and Levi are okay but what about McKayla?"

His dad rubbed his hand over his face. "She's missing. They think she might have wandered away from the wreck."

Later that afternoon his dad had left with ten other Wolves to go look for their missing member. A search that had finally ended fifteen years later when he'd watched that asshole lead Mac into the auditorium on a leash three days ago.

A hand on his shoulder made him jump.

"You okay, brother?" Harley asked him. "We're about ready to sit down to dinner."

"Uh, yeah. Just got lost in my memories for a bit." He turned to face his friend. "When you have some free time, we should talk."

"I've got some time tomorrow morning, we can talk about what you found out about Gladieux and the Black Paw Pack.

Mac

She tried to hide her yawn behind her hand but Harley saw it. Furtively, she'd watched how the others interacted – she'd never really been able to observe a real family. And that's what she saw here, a family. She told them of her experiences growing up in the system, trying to gloss over how terrified she'd been when her Wolf had awakened and started talking to her. They all scowled when she talked about the visits to therapists and how she'd been treated as being defective.

The dinner dishes had been cleared away and they all had bottles of beer or cups of coffee sitting in front of them. "It's been a long day," The Alpha said as he winked at her, at least she thought he was winking at her. "I'm sure McKayla would like a shower and a soft bed after a couple of nights out in the woods."

She nodded, so tired it was hard to hold her eyes open. The carb-heavy meal had tasted wonderful but it had made her sleepy.

"Levi, would you show McKayla to her room?"

At her slight frown he corrected himself, "I mean Mac. Whatever you want to be called, you are wanted here and this is your home."

She allowed him to give her another long hug. Surprised when he kissed the top of her head, she stepped back and looked up at him. He was even taller than Brock.

"Sorry if I made you feel uncomfortable. I remember Dad doing that to us before we traipsed up to bed and I thought…"

"It felt nice. I'm just not used to…" she trailed off as she tried to think of the right word, "affection."

Levi scowled and opened the door. "This is your room. We kept it exactly the same, we knew someday you would come home to us."

She stepped into the room and stopped. It felt so familiar. Spying a stuffed dog on the bed she hurried over and picked it up and hugged it. "Charleykins!" This one small thing she remembered helped her feel like maybe she did belong here.

Brock

Following Harley to The Alpha's office at the back of the house, Brock tried to figure out how to broach the subject of his accidental mating to Mac.

He stared at the picture of Harley and Levi with his dad just before Harley assumed his role as The Alpha. The clink of a bottle against a glass caught his attention.

Harley held out a glass to him. "You look as if you want to puke so it must be bad."

"Not bad, exactly. Well, yeah, maybe bad," he stated before he gulped the bourbon. Rolling the glass between his hands he blurted out. "I'm mated to Mac."

"Did you just say what I think you said?" Harley asked as he stared at his face. "You are MATED to my SISTER?" Forgoing the glass in his hand he gulped bourbon straight from the bottle.

"It was an accident…"

Harley interrupted him with a growled, "You don't 'accidentally' get mated."

Now Brock really felt like he was going to puke. He'd known it would be bad and he'd been right about that. Watching Harley pace the length of the desk and turn glare at him, he knew this was a monumental test of their friendship. "I'd been poisoned by a wolfsbane coated bullet."

"What? Who? Oh, Gladieux, I should have known." He poured Brock another couple of fingers of bourbon. "Drink that and then start at the beginning."

Brock threw back the drink and swallowed hard, the burn of the alcohol against his throat brought his focus to the man staring at him. He was mad, sure, and for good reason but there was also concern on his face. Concern for his friend, his sister, and for his pack. "It started when I watched one of Gladieux's men lead Mac into the auditorium on a leash."

"What the actual fuck!" he roared as his fingernails started to turn into claws. Brock watched his friend struggle to calm himself. "Sorry, just the thought of Wolves using leashes…"

"It gets worse." He held the glass out for more of the alcohol. "The collar and ropes were soaked with wolfsbane."

Harley's glass hit the wall with a crash. "Go on," he said through gritted teeth.

Brock's Wolf whined and he reassured him that things would be okay. "At first they were trying to get her to reveal her lineage and wouldn't believe her when she told them she had no pack."

Harley stood at the end of the desk, his hands flat on the top with his head bowed. "How did we not know this was going on? How many other..." He stood tall and ran his hands through his hair. "We'll figure that out later. I need to hear the rest of your explanation."

"I convinced Gladieux to give Mac to me and I took her back to my house where I treated her wounds. Her eyes haunted me for some reason and then when I got close enough to really see her, I knew. There was no mistaking that she was your sister."

Harley sat in one of the chairs, slouching as if all the steel had gone out of him. "Why didn't you leave then?"

"Gladieux had his men watching me. I'd mostly gained his trust but I think he knew something about me wasn't how it looked. I showed Mac to the spare bedroom. I had a devil of a time keeping her from trying to run away." He sat across from his friend before continuing. "The next morning in the auditorium they questioned us and told us about the fealty and mating ceremonies that were to take place later that day. After cleaning up and getting Mac something appropriate to wear, we went back. We had to go through the mating cere-mony, if we hadn't he probably would have had us executed on the spot. I tried to keep the bite soft but my Wolf had other ideas." He smiled sadly. "We were outed when Mac forgot and called me by my real name and we had to run. She got away and my Wolf led them away from her. I took a bullet to the shoulder and somehow found my way to Mac and Mitch.

I was in the throes of wolfsbane poisoning so Mitch drew them away from us and Mac found us a hiding spot. The rest I can only guess at as everything is a bit hazy and I was out of it for a while. When I woke the next morning, I felt the pain of the mating tattoo scribing itself into my flesh."

Harley sighed. "For now, until we figure things out, stay away from Mac."

"Okay, but my Wolf isn't going to be happy about it. He insists we're fated mates."

"As it wasn't entirely your fault as you were under the influence of wolfsbane, I'll have to figure out a suitable punishment for the unapproved mating. On the other hand, I owe you everything for returning our sister to us."

"Oh, and I think Gladieux has other prisoners, and Mac said something about sensing a pup in the dungeon."

"He's got a pup? I haven't heard anything about any kidnappings. I'll get my men on it." Harley pulled his phone out of his pocket and sent a text. After a sharp knock on the door, Levi stepped into the room.

At the look on his brother's face, Levi stood tall. "Yes, Alpha?"

"Call a meeting of all the warriors for eight am tomorrow, there's a definite problem with Gladieux, just as we suspected."

As Beta, Levi handled all the logistics of getting meetings set and Wolves where they needed to be.

"Now, Levi, I have other things, family things, to discuss with you."

Levi poured himself a drink and sat when his brother motioned to the other chair. "Brock, go shower and sleep. Tomorrow will be a long day. I need you at that meeting in the morning to discuss everything you witnessed."

"Yes, Alpha," he replied before walking to the door. He

opened the door and stepped into the hallway as he heard Harley telling Levi about the mating.

"He what?" Levi snapped as he closed the door behind him.

Trudging up the stairs he wondered how this would affect the long-standing friendship between him and The Alpha and Beta.

Ten minutes later he was standing in the shower, gloriously hot water pounding on his sore muscles and his thoughts turned to his mate, Mac, and he caught himself wondering if her hair was the same fiery red it had been when she was a child. Turning the faucet handles to cold he hoped a blast of icy water would clear his head of thoughts of her.

Chapter Eight

Mac

S he picked at the skin around one of her fingernails, wincing as the skin tore away, leaving a bloody spot. *It will be okay*, her Wolf told her. *Brock's wolf is right, it's fated.*

"How do you know?" she whispered out loud.

Nearly jumping out of her skin at the sharp knock on her door, she rubbed her damp palms on her jeans and wished for the rest of her clothes that were left somewhere out in the woods.

"Coming," she said as another sharp knock broke the quiet of the early morning.

She opened the door to find Levi standing there with his hands in his jacket pockets. "You want some breakfast? I thought you might want to eat before the meeting."

"I don't know if I'll be able to eat anything," she admitted. "It was bad enough with just the family last night. I don't know if I'm ready to be the focus of that many…"

Levi pulled her in for a hug. "I get it, the whole pack

together can be intimidating but they are just an extension of our family. At least that's true for this pack, I can't speak for most other packs." He set her away from him. "Let's go. It'll be okay, I swear. Mostly just a bunch of speeches and then food and drink. It's not that big a deal."

Looking at him, horror plain on her face, she whispered, "Speeches? I going to have to make a speech?"

He took her hand in his and she was grateful for the warmth, her hands had gone ice cold. "You don't have to speak unless you want to. Harley will be the one making the speech." He pulled her toward the stairs. "And he's good at it. I'm glad he's The Alpha and not me," he admitted to her. "Not that I admit that out loud to anyone so keep that between you and me."

She smiled up at him and continued down the stairs.

The kitchen was warm and smelled of bacon and coffee. Harley stood at the stove, a fork in his hand. "Coffee's hot and bacon will be done soon. Scrambled eggs okay with everyone?"

Mac nodded and grimaced when her stomach rumbled loudly. With a giggle she made her way to the coffee pot and poured a cup, adding creamer from the bottle sitting on the counter. Sipping at her coffee she choked on a sip when Brock walked into the room, his hair still damp from his shower. She frowned at the bluish moons under his eyes, as if he hadn't slept.

His gaze zeroed in on her and he smiled. "Morning, Mac."

She blushed and took a sip from her mug as her thoughts went to how those lips felt against her skin.

Sauntering over to the counter he reached above her for a mug out of the cupboard. His unique scent tickled her nose and sent a zing of awareness through her body, making her want to slide up to him and wrap her arms around him. She looked up at him and he turned his gaze away from her.

"Levi, everything ready for the meeting? Need help?" He moved away from her and took a seat at the table next to Levi.

"No, my guys have it handled."

Harley turned from the stove, a platter of bacon in one hand and another piled high with fluffy scrambled eggs in the other. "Now remember, we have a female at the table now." He smacked Levi's hand when he reached for a piece of bacon. "I wasn't done talking yet. Let McKa... I mean Mac, get some first before you guys inhale everything."

Levi motioned for Mac to fill her plate. "He's right, we tend to forget about anyone else when it comes to food." He snuck a piece of bacon and stuffed it in his mouth as she was scooping some eggs onto her plate. "Especially with bacon," he said after he swallowed.

Once her plate was filled, the others filled their plates until even the crumbs were gone.

She looked at Brock sitting directly across the table from her. "You okay, Brock?"

"Yeah," he snapped before standing and putting his plate in the sink. He hurried out of the room and she frowned. What was up with that? He acted like he couldn't hardly stand to reply to her question.

She finished up her breakfast, surprised she'd been able to eat all that food. Picking up her plate she went to place it in the dishwasher when Levi stopped her and took the plate from her hand.

"Let me," he said as he turned and put the plate in the dishwasher for her. He pulled her over to the window, away from his brother. "I know Harley won't think of this so... I noticed you didn't have anything other than the small pack with you. I can take you to the mall and get you some new clothes."

She could feel the heat rising in her cheeks. Not having much was her normal but obviously it wasn't for her newly found family. "I don't have any money. If you show me where the washer and dryer are I could…"

Levi interrupted her, "I just thought you'd like something appropriate to wear to the meeting today."

Horrified, she looked down at the floor and mumbled, "Maybe I should just stay here." Brushing at a tear of frustration, she turned to run out of the room.

"McKay… shit, I mean Mac, please don't be offended. Obviously, you worked hard for what you have."

"And I can't afford anything else right now. If you'll lend me some money I'm sure I can find something suitable at a thrift shop. You do have one of these here, don't you?"

"That's not necessary, Mac. You've got plenty of money."

She looked at him quizzically. "What do you mean?"

He took her hand and held it in his. "As a member of the Jensen family you are entitled to a share of the company profits.

"What company? What are you talking about?"

"The pack owns the most popular restaurant and bar in town. Half of the profits go to a fund to help any pack member who needs it. The other half goes to the ruling family. Harley has been depositing your share in an account for you every year."

"But I haven't done anything to deserve…"

He pulled out his phone and brought up the bank website, punching in the information needed to log in. A couple more taps and he showed her the screen.

She gasped at the number. "Is that right? Surely that's for all three of us."

"No, that's yours. Your share has been deposited every year since you were born." He shoved the phone back into his pocket. "If nothing else, we need to go to the bank and get your access to the account. Until then, I can float you a loan."

She hugged him. "Thanks for being so nice to me." She didn't see how Levi's jaw went hard.

Brock

He stopped just outside the kitchen and leaned against the wall, his head hanging down. It was only the first morning and his Wolf was growling at him. He'd promised Harley he'd stay away from Mac, at least for a while until they could figure out what to do about the unauthorized mating. His Wolf couldn't care less about the promise he'd made to his Alpha, he just wanted to be near Mac. Maybe Harley had another assignment for him away from the pack. When he heard the dishwasher open, he hurried upstairs before Mac could come along and discover him lurking about. Surely, either Harley or Levi had explained how the accidental mating would have to be undone. He really needed to get away and find a willing female to take out some of this sexual tension. Maybe then he could be around Mac without wanting to drag her to a quiet corner and have his way with her again. Just the thought of her hands on his skin had him heading for his shower. Maybe some ice-cold water would put this fire in his blood out for a while.

Two hours later and he was pulling his good shirt out of the closet. Pack meetings were an occasion, requiring something more than a t-shirt and dirty jeans. He frowned at the shirt, the wrinkles in the fabric unacceptable. With a grumble he pulled out the ironing board and iron, going to the fridge for a beer while he waited for the appliance to heat up.

As he ironed, he let his mind wander, ironing was soothing in a way he'd never understood. The swish the iron made as he moved it over the fabric calmed his rattled nerves. How was he going to stay away from Mac? Harley had hinted at a big project for him, he hoped it would be enough to take his mind off of the pink-haired female who'd captured the interest of his Wolf after just one look.

Satisfied that the shirt was now wrinkle-free, he pulled it on as he unplugged the iron.

As he buttoned the shirt, he went over the plan with his Wolf. *Now, we have to stay away from Mac.* He grinned at his Wolf's grumble. *I know, but it's an order from our Alpha so we have to try.*

He glanced at the clock. *Better get a move on. I've got to stop and see Mom before the meeting.*

Five minutes later he pulled into the driveway of his childhood home, which happened to be next door to the Jensen's. Jingling his keys in his hand, he ambled up the walk, turning to look when he heard a truck pull into the Jensen's driveway.

Jacked up and loud, the truck stopped by the sidewalk. He couldn't help himself, he watched the driver side door open and a guy he didn't recognize got out and trotted over to the passenger side to help his passenger out of the truck. The door shut and his Wolf went berserk when he caught sight of the distinctive pink hair. The red roots were gone and her hair looked sleek and professionally styled.

"Calm your shit," he muttered to his Wolf as he tried to turn away. He was under his Alpha's orders to stay away from her. Mac turned back and noticed him and waved, a huge smile on her face.

He gave a nod in response, grateful he was wearing his

sunglasses so she couldn't see how his eyes were trained on the guy next to her.

Her shoulders dropped at his lackluster greeting and she turned and walked into the house.

Stretching his neck, he turned back to his parent's house and made his way up the front walk.

"Mom? It's Brock."

He closed the door behind him and followed the sound of his mother's voice. "He just got here. I'll tell him." She waved him over to the kitchen island and set a glass of iced tea in front of him. "Yes, we'll be there soon. Love you."

Placing her phone on the counter, she frowned at him. "What's wrong? And don't tell me nothing, I'm your mother and I can tell something is bothering you."

He smiled sadly at her as she pulled a bottle of rum out of the cupboard.

"You look like you need something stronger than sweet tea," she said as she held up the bottle.

"No thanks, Ma, I better not. I might not stop at one drink." It would take more than one drink for the alcohol to affect him but the mood he was in he didn't want to start, showing up drunk to a pack meeting would be bad and he was already in trouble for the unapproved mating.

"Okay then. Does it have something to do with the unap-proved mating?"

His head snapped up. "Who told you?"

"Never mind who told me. The question is why did I have to hear it from someone other than you?"

"Shit," he mumbled as he ran his hands over his face. "We got into town and we went straight to the Jensen's being as she is their missing sister. We had dinner and then I went home."

"You couldn't dial that phone in your pocket and call us?" She stood in front of him and looked up into his face.

He couldn't help but smile, the top of her head barely reached his shoulder. She was tiny for a Wolf but she made up for it in attitude which was currently directed at him. "I... uh... I don't know." He picked her up in a hug.

"Put me down, you big lug. Just like your father," she said with a laugh as he put her feet back on the floor. "Tell me about her. I should know everything about my daughter-in-law."

"Don't get too excited. Harley may declare the mating void as it was not approved. It was actually kinda an accident."

"You don't accidentally get mated. Explain. Now."

He told her everything, starting with seeing her led into the room on a leash all the way to their arrival at the Jensen house the previous night.

"Oh, well, that's interesting. Your Wolf is sure it's fated?"

"Yep, and he's being very vocal about it too. He saw another Wolf helping her out of a truck when I got here and it was all I could do to keep him from coming forward and claiming his territory."

"Okay then, we'll need to convince Harley that the mating should be allowed." She picked up her phone. "Now, get to the meeting, I've got plans to make."

He rubbed his hands over his face and sighed. Now that his mom was involved, who knew what was going to happen next? He was out the door before he remembered she was supposed to tell him something.

Mac

At the mall Mac had looked around at all the stores and

wanted to run back out to the truck, Levi had left her in the care of a young Wolf named Cody with instructions to buy an outfit for the pack meeting and a new phone.

Cody put his hand at her back and waited for her to calm down.

She looked around, the number of people wandering around the open space had her questioning if the mall was such a good idea. What if one of Gladieux's men spotted her?

"Hey, you okay?" Cody asked her as he took her hand.

"Yeah, there's just so many people here."

"Just remember, if The Alpha thought there was any kind of threat he wouldn't have let us come here alone."

"That's true," she admitted, "Harley does seem to be extremely protective."

He pulled her down past the big department store and into a small boutique. "I think you might find something here. My sister loves this store though she does complain that they're more expensive."

She ran her hand over some dresses hanging on the wall. "How dressy is this meeting? I know it won't be ball gowns but…"

"I keep forgetting you don't know how things work. The women use it as an excuse to dress up so a dress would be good." He pointed to a skirt on a rack. "Something like that would work."

She picked up the skirt and examined it, trying not to let her shock at the price on the tag show. There was quite a large sum of money in the account that Levi had shown her, more than she could spend over a few years. She'd tried to hand the card linked to the account back to him but he wouldn't take it. "This money is yours due to your birthright, spend it however you wish."

Deciding to buy the skirt she started searching for a blouse to wear with it.

She was ready for a nap by the time they got done at the mobile phone store, a brand new smartphone in her purse. As they walked through the mall, she found herself staring at her reflection in the store windows, wondering who it was staring back at her. Her hair styled and freshly dyed a deep pink, she didn't feel like herself.

"Oh no, I didn't realize it was getting so late. We better get back so I can get ready."

"Don't worry, they won't start without you. The meeting is to introduce you to the pack. Hard to start without the guest of honor."

She stared out the window and swallowed, hoping the butterflies in her stomach would stay where they were. By the time they'd gotten to the phone store she was using the card without a qualm, the money had become something useful instead of something needed to survive.

As they'd pulled up into the driveway, she noticed Brock standing next to a huge truck, way bigger than the one she was riding in. It was so big she wondered if she'd be able to get in without using a stepladder. Excited to see Brock she practically jumped out of the truck when Cody opened her door. Waving madly, she was distressed to see he only nodded curtly before going into the house. She brought her hand down dejectedly, wondering what she'd done wrong. And why was he at the house next door? *Oh wait, that must be his parents'*. She thought she remembered someone saying something about them living next door last night. Following Cody into her brother's house she wiped at a tear before anyone else could see. Trying to explain feelings that she didn't understand herself wasn't on her list of things she wanted to do that day.

She looked at the time and grimaced, she only had thirty minutes before the pack started to arrive. At least her hair was done, the stylist had wanted to dye it back to her natural color but Mac wasn't ready for that. She did let her dye it a darker pink. Hiding behind her pink hair was her safety net.

After a quick shower she used some of the makeup she'd purchased, watching a video on how to apply it first even though it was just a little mascara and blush.

Now, as she stood in front of the full-length mirror in the bathroom, she thought she looked passable, it would take some time before she was comfortable with the makeup and hair routine. Her life was going to be so very different from what she was used to.

She looked over when a knock sounded on her bedroom door. Probably her brother wondering what was taking her so long.

Harley stood in the hallway, his back to her and his phone to his ear. That reminded her to grab her phone and put it in her purse. Her purse, she never thought she'd be carrying a purse instead of the backpack.

He finished his call and turned around, his eyes going wide as he took in her new outfit. "Wow, you clean up nice."

"Is it okay? I've never worn a skirt before, I hope I don't fall off these shoes and embarrass you," she said as she motioned to the heels.

"It's perfect," he replied. "I wanted to talk to you about something before we join the rest of the pack."

"Oh, did I do something wrong? Levi assured me I was able to use the money…"

"It's not about the money, I'm glad it was there for you to use. I wanted to talk to you about your Mating."

"My Mating? I'm not Mated."

"Actually, you are. Didn't your Wolf tell you?"

"No, but she has seemed very satisfied with herself the last couple of days, ever since Brock and I..." Her mouth opened and nothing else came out. "You mean, that because we, I... oh shit."

"You didn't feel the mating tattoo burning itself into your skin?"

She rubbed her hands up and down her arms, suddenly freezing. "Yeah, but I thought it was a sunburn or something. He told me he would keep his Wolf from biting hard enough to ..." Her mind whirled with the possibilities. "He's not in trouble is he? I mean, I was the one who kinda took advantage of his fever and threw myself at him."

"Well..." he drew out the word as he thought about an appropriate response. "I haven't decided. As his Alpha the mating should have been approved prior to the event but it happens." He picked up her hand and held it in both of his. "Once I learned the circumstances of how you grew up, I just want for you to have the choice whether or not to be mated."

"I don't want him to be punished for something I did." Her cheeks grew hot and she stared down at her shoes. "What we did felt special. I guess I'm just confused."

"Confused about what? Sex?"

"Geez, no. And I don't want to talk to my brother about that." She made a disgusted face and shook her head. "I'm confused about whether it was the right thing to do. It felt right, but..." her voice trailed off as she looked out the window and saw Brock getting in his truck. "Oh, never mind. I just need to think about things for a while." The flash of longing and anger she'd felt at just the sight of Brock made her wonder. What if she felt the same for another Wolf? Or was it just Brock?

Chapter Nine

Brock

H e wandered through the auditorium, alert for any Wolf who looked nervous or out of place. Now that they were on Gladieux's radar who knew what that crazy fucker would do?

He sauntered over to Levi who was stationed at the entrance welcoming people.

"Is he here yet?" Brock asked when there was a break in the people streaming into the auditorium.

"I believe he's in the lounge working on his speech."

"Thanks," Brock said as he turned away and strode toward the back. The door to the lounge was open a crack and he heard his friend's voice as he practiced. "And thank you to Brock Atkinson for bringing our McKayla back to us." His tone changed and he said to himself, "should I mention the mating and that it's not approved?"

"What the actual fuck, dude" Brock practically growled, not caring that he was talking to The Alpha. The man standing in front of him was, in his mind, his best friend first.

"Do you realize you are the only person besides my brother and sister that can talk to me like that without being punished?" He sat and looked up at his best friend. "You've been there for me, for both me and Levi really, through everything. If Levi wasn't my Beta I'd want you in that position."

Brock stared down at him in disbelief. "Then why don't you want me mated to Mac? Surely matings have been done without prior approval before?"

"It's not that the mating was not approved," Harley admitted, "it's that we didn't get a chance to know her as our sister before she became your mate."

His wolf wanted to jump up and down with glee. "So, if I let you all get to know her without any interference from me, you'll let the mating stand?"

Harley motioned for him to sit. "Park it, you're giving me a crick in my neck looking up at you."

Brock sat and ran his hands through his hair, waiting for Harley to answer his question.

"Right now, all I can say is maybe. I need to think about it some more and talk to Levi about it, she's his sister too so he should have a say. And, I want to discuss it with McKayla, she may not understand what being mated means."

Brock slouched into the chair, his muscles finally relaxing. He hadn't realized he'd been holding himself so rigid. He was almost positive that Mac would want the mating to stand.

"I also have to consider how it will look if I let the mating stand without the proper length of time to consider it."

"Thanks, man," he said as he stood.

Harley glanced at his phone before shoving it into his back pocket. "It's time," he said as a knock sounded on the door.

The door creaked open slowly. "Brother, it's time," Levi

said as he looked from his brother to his friend. "You two good?"

"Yeah," Harley growled, now in The Alpha mode, "let's do this."

They made their way onto the raised stage, Harley first, then Levi, and Brock after him as Wolf Law dictated.

Levi stepped to the front of the stage as Harley and Brock waited, relaxed and at ease.

Levi quieted the crowd and motioned to Harley.

"Thank you all for showing up today, I know this pack meeting was just announced yesterday afternoon. We had something huge happen yesterday that needs to be shared." He glanced back at Brock. "As all of you know our sister was lost to us on the day our parents were killed and we've been searching for her ever since. Well, you've probably already heard the rumors that she has returned to us. The rumors are true, thanks to Brock Atkinson who discovered McKayla while he was on assignment for this pack. Our sister is now back with us." He motioned to Brock's father who led Mac up to the stage.

With a nod to him, Harley continued his speech as he took her hand in his. "This is McKayla, she's going to need some time to adjust. She prefers to be called Mac. We'll have a formal welcome home party in two weeks after the annual fealty ceremony. That will give her time to get settled into our pack."

A voice rose in the crowd. "Where was she all this time? Is another pack responsible?"

Harley knew someone would want to know more. "We are investigating. We will have a special meeting when we have all the facts."

Chapter Ten

Mac

As soon as Harley indicated the meeting was over, the female pack members retreated to the kitchen to set out the sandwiches and salads to feed the hungry pack. Mac watched as her brothers sauntered to the back of the room as the rest of the pack broke into smaller groups as they discussed what they'd just heard. The warriors argued amongst themselves as to who The Alpha would pick to head up the group that would be heading to Ankton to meet with Gladieux and his pack.

Her attention shifted to Harley as he talked with Brock and Levi, his face showing his frustration. She walked up and heard Brock practically growling at her brothers. "No, I do not agree."

Harley frowned until he caught sight of her walking up behind Brock. She watched as he smiled, but she could tell it was forced.

"Mac," he said he made a motion with his hand to Brock

and Levi to stop their heated discussion. "I hope you are settling in okay."

"Yes, thank you," she replied nervously as she watched Brock through her lashes. "You said you needed to discuss something with me after the meeting."

He held his hand out to his sister. "Yes, and we should do that in private. Why don't we grab some food and take it to my office?"

Brock scowled until he noticed Mac's gaze come back to him. "I think I should…"

"No," Harley interrupted him. "I need to talk with Mac alone."

Brock's shoulders slumped slightly as he turned away.

Harley put his hand on Brock's shoulder to stop him. "I've got another assignment for you, come find me later."

With a nod in acknowledgement, Brock walked away toward a group of warriors.

Once their turn at the table of food came, Mac stood and stared at the array of food spread out before her, wondering how she was going to pick what to eat.

Harley reached in front of her and selected a sandwich. "I know, it's a lot." He looked at her. "Ham or turkey?"

"Ham," she replied and watched as he placed a sandwich on her plate.

He scooped up some potato salad and plopped it on her plate. "This is the best, you'll thank me later."

Once their plates were full, he led her to his office and closed the door. "I hope you're settling in okay."

"Yes. Thank you for having Cody take me shopping. I'd have hated to be underdressed for the meeting today since you're the Alpha. I mean, I don't want to disappoint you."

"McKa… Mac, I could never be disappointed in you, you're my sister. I know it's going to take a while for you to

feel completely comfortable here after the way you grew up."
His eyes flared bright green for a moment. "I would give
anything for you to not have to have gone through that. And I
know Levi feels the same."

"I'm going to try so hard to not disappoint you. I know I
have so much to…"

He put down his sandwich. "You could never disappoint
me, Mac."

She let out a long breath. "I'm not used to living with so
many people around watching me. I'm sure I'm going to
screw up." She tried to hold back the tears but just the
thought of making her brother look bad to the pack had her
on the verge of freaking out. As a tear fell, she watched
Harley jump up and hurry around the desk to go down on one
knee in front of her.

"Hey, Mac, don't cry," he said as he brushed her hair back
behind her ear and out of her face.

"I'm sorry," she sobbed as she brushed the offending tears
away angrily. "I don't want to have the pack look down on
you because I don't know…" She took a deep breath and
tried to compose herself. "I could feel them all staring at me
at the meeting."

"They were curious about where you've been is all. No
one in our pack would judge you." He picked her up from the
chair and sat in it himself, settling her on his lap.

She leaned against him and let the steady beat of his heart
under her ear sooth her. "This feels…" she took a minute,
trying to force herself to remember, "familiar."

He kissed the top of her head. "I used to do this when you
were tired and fighting a nap. Somehow, I could always get
you to relax enough to fall asleep." He leaned back in the
chair and rubbed his hand up and down her back, as he had
when she was small. "Mom would always bring you to me

73

when you were upset or overtired as I could always get you calmed down."

She sat there in his lap and let him soothe away her fears. When her eyelids grew heavy, she forced herself to sit up and look at him.

"Thank you, Lele."

He grinned hugely. "You remember!"

"I remember bits and pieces, but mostly just feelings. Like how I felt just now."

She stood up and brushed the wrinkles out of her skirt. "Now, you wanted to talk to me about something." She motioned for him to return to his seat across the desk from her.

"Yes." He cleared his throat. "I, uh, need, no want, to talk to you about being mated to Brock."

Her mind immediately went rushing off, fearing the worst. "He's not in trouble, is he? Because it wasn't his fault, it was mine."

"How was it your fault you're mated? From my understanding it takes two," he commented with a smirk.

"Well, yeah, but Brock was out of it from the bullet wound. My wolf took over insisting we're fated. Not that I know exactly what that means."

"A wolf can fall in love and mate with a wolf of their choosing but a fated mate is something entirely different. According to the stories passed down from our ancestors a fated mate is special and not every wolf has a fated mate." He folded his hands in front of him on the desk. "As The Alpha, all matings are supposed to be approved by me ahead of time."

"Are you going to reverse the mating?"

"I do have that authority."

She frowned, "If it's not a true mating how come I've got his mark on me?"

"Now wait, I haven't decided about your mating yet. I wanted to make sure it was something you actually wanted and not just because you thought you had to…"

"I don't know. I've never even dated, how would I know anything about mating? Do I have to decide right now?"

He smiled. "No, you can take all the time you need. I'm sending Brock off on another assignment in a couple of days so you'll feel more free to maybe meet some other wolves and get acclimated to pack life."

A knock at the office door interrupted him. "Yes?"

Brock's mother poked her head into the room. "Sorry to disturb you, Harley, but are you going to keep your sister all to yourself all afternoon? I have some wolves her age I want to introduce her to. Even she needs some friends her own age."

She smiled at the woman, remembering how welcoming she'd been when Brock had introduced her to his parents. His mother had immediately swept her up into a familiar feeling hug. She'd smelled of fresh air and sunshine, a smell that tickled at her memory.

"Of course, Mrs. Atkinson." Harley turned back to Mac. "Now, think about what I said. Go, have fun."

Mac followed the older woman out of the office, her heart thumping crazily in her chest at the thought of meeting more new people.

When they stopped at a group of young wolves, Mac looked down at her shoes as Mrs. Atkinson introduced her to the group.

"I like your blouse. I almost bought it but now I'm glad I didn't."

Mac looked up as the girl continued, "it looks way better on you than it did on me."

Another girl piped up, "Was it hard to get your hair that color? I've been wanting to go with a green stripe but my mom is against it."

At first only giving single word answers, she eventually relaxed enough to enjoy being in the company of girls she could become friends with. Being shuffled from foster home to foster home, Mac hadn't made any real friends.

The next day, Mac looked through her small collection of clothes, wondering what to wear to go out with her new friends to the mall. Should she dress up? Or jeans and a tee? Those were her only two options until she did some more shopping.

A tap on the door had her glancing at her phone for the time. "Crap," she muttered as she hurried over to open the door. "I know I'm late," she said as she pulled at the hem of her shirt, "I couldn't decide what to wear."

When Sherry didn't reply she looked up, shocked to discover it wasn't her new friend. It was Brock, his eyes focused her.

"Oh," she gasped as her hand went to her throat. "I was expecting someone else."

"Obviously," he said with a grin.

Her stomach churned and her hands wanted to shake as the scent of him wafted over her. She wanted nothing more than to snuggle into him but she knew she shouldn't until her brother made his decision about their mating.

"Oh, hey Brock. What's up? I don't really have time to…"

He interrupted. "Get ready for what?"

"I'm going to the mall with some Wolves my age."

"I'm glad you're still here. I wanted to talk to you before I leave."

"You're leaving? Why?" she shook her head. "Never mind, that's none of my business." He'd ignored her at the ceremony the day before and that still stung. She stared down at her bare feet, hoping he liked the bright pink nail polish on her toes.

"The Alpha is sending me with Levi to check out a rumor that the son of the White Paw Alpha is missing."

"Do you think it's the pup I felt being held by Gladieux?"

"Maybe. That's why Harley is sending me along as I've personally dealt with Gladieux and his men."

"That makes sense," she said as she turned around to look for her shoes. "Be careful," she said as she bent over to look under the bed, reaching for the shoes she found under there.

"I, uh, wanted to make sure you're okay being here with your brothers."

She stood and turned back to face him, her shoes dangling from her fingers. "Yeah, I'm good." Still a bit miffed at his ignoring her the day before she dismissed him. "I hope you find the pup. Now, I've got to get ready, I'm sure Sherry is getting anxious and wondering when I'm going to be ready. Thanks for stopping by."

Hoping she was outwardly looking way calmer than she felt, she sauntered to the dresser and opened a drawer to pull out a clean pair of socks.

"Hey, Brock," she heard Sherry say.

"Hi, Sherry," he replied as he looked down at her face. "How's your mom?"

"She's good now that Stevie has settled down with a mate."

Brock reached down and ran a lock of Sherry's hair through his fingers. "I like the blonde, it suits you."

Mac watched and wished she felt as calm around Brock as her friend looked, her cheeks going pink when Brock caught her staring.

"See ya later, Mac. If you need anything let my mom know."

She looked at him through her lashes. "Okay."

After they heard him go down the stairs Sherry giggled and waved her hand at her face. "Wow, Mac, how'd you be around him alone out in the woods and not climb him like a tree?"

Mac's mouth dropped open in shock at her question. Her brother had told her they were keeping the mating a secret from most of the pack until he made his decision.

"Well, he was hurt, and…"

"I'm kidding," she said as Mac turned to go sit on the bed to put on her shoes and socks.

When she sat on the bed she looked up to discover Sherry staring at her.

"No wonder," Sherry muttered.

"What? Is something hanging out that shouldn't be?" she asked as she checked her clothing. And then she realized part of the mating tattoo was showing.

"You're already mated. To who?"

When Mac's face went red, she guessed.

"Brock? You're mated to the most eligible Wolf, besides your brothers, of the Red Tail Pack?"

"It's not like that," she mumbled as she looked down at the floor. Reminding herself she wasn't the weird outsider anymore she looked up and said, "it was a bit of an accident, the mating, I mean."

Sherry grinned at her. "You don't get mated by accident."

"Yeah, well, we did. We're just waiting to see if Harley

approves the mating since it was done without his knowledge."

"The Alpha didn't know? How in the hell does that happen?"

"Told you, it was an accident." She didn't want to go into an explanation of what happened so she turned and started to walk toward the door. "You coming?"

Her new friend followed behind her as she walked toward the waiting truck, Cody leaning against the fender.

"Hey, Mac, Sherry," he acknowledged the two girls. "You guys ready to go?"

Two hours later Mac ambled toward the food court, her stomach rumbling. "Who else is hungry?"

Cody followed behind them, his hands full of bags of the girl's purchases. "Yeah, this pack wolf needs a drink."

"I told you we'd be fine while you took the bags out to the truck," Mac said as she took in all the choices of varieties of food.

"Your brother told me not to leave you alone so that's what I'm doing.

"He's a big worrywart." She dropped her purse on the table. "I want pizza."

Cody piped up, "Me too."

"Cool, I'll order a whole pie. You want pizza, Sherry?"

"Sure," her friend said as she pulled out her wallet.

"I'll get it," Mac said as she walked toward the pizza place. "I hope you both like pepperoni and mushroom."

She returned to the table and plopped into the empty chair. "It should be done in a few minutes."

"We were talking about going to Moonbeam tonight. You want to go with?" Sherry asked excitedly.

"What is Moonbeam? A restaurant or something?" A voice calling out their order number took her attention from

Sherry and she didn't see the pointed look her friend sent at Cody.

"That's our pizza, I'll be right back." As she walked back toward the pizza place, she heard Cody say "Ow" and she looked back to see Sherry gesturing wildly as she talked to him. "I wonder what that is all about?" she mumbled to her wolf as she picked up their food.

"I don't trust Sherry, her Wolf smells of deceit," her Wolf said back to her.

"I'm sure you're mistaken," she said to placate her Wolf. "They don't know me and I don't really know them. I'll be careful."

With a chuff her Wolf backed off, grumbling.

When she returned to the table she looked from Sherry to Cody. "What's going on?"

"Oh, nothing," Sherry chirped as she stared at Cody as if daring him to object.

Once they were all happily munching on pizza, Sherry brought up the mysterious Moonbeam again. "Back to our conversation from before, Moonbeam is the place for young wolves to hang out."

Chapter Eleven

Mac

When they'd walked up to the door of Moonbeam dance music wrapped around them every time the door opened to admit more Wolves. Once they were inside, Mac stopped and stared around as the lights from the ceiling above the dance floor pulsed to the beat of the music.

Sherry pulled Mac to an open table. Cody asked what they wanted to drink.

"Beer," sherry said as Mac stared at her. Surely, they weren't twenty-one, she thought. "Don't worry, it's okay. Young Wolves are allowed beer once they're sixteen as it doesn't affect us the same as it does humans. It just makes us a little more relaxed."

Even so, Mac still requested a soda as her brother hadn't told her she was allowed.

Cody pushed his way through the crowd toward the bar to get their drinks. Sherry clapped her hands. "Oh, look at all the good looking Wolves here tonight. This will be fun."

Heat from the lights and bodies on the dance floor wafted over them, making Mac glad she'd listened to Sherry and hadn't changed out of the tank top.

"Here you go," Cody said as he set the glass of soda in front of her. "You want to dance?"

Mac smiled. "Not yet, I just want to watch for a while. You guys go ahead."

Mac twirled the straw in her soda between her fingers as she watched her new friends dancing to the music blasting from the speakers at each side of the stage. They looked like they were having fun and she had almost talked herself into joining them when she heard a voice from behind her.

"Are you here alone?"

She looked up as the owner of the voice stepped closer. "No, my friends are dancing."

"A pretty Wolf like you shouldn't be left on her own in here, there's a lot of creeps that hang out looking for vulnerable females." He sat in the chair next to her. "I'm Sean."

"Mac."

"Unusual name for a girl." He commented.

"It's short for McKayla."

Her wolf chuffed at her. "*He's cute but he's not Brock.*"

"*Shush, Brock's not here and I just want to have a little fun,*" she thought to her wolf.

"Would you like to dance?" he asked, holding his hand out to her.

She knew Brock wouldn't be happy but surely one dance wouldn't hurt anything. "Okay," she said. She put her hand in his and stood.

His hand was warm as his fingers gripped hers as he led her to the dance floor.

Mac shuffled her feet back and forth to the beat and let the music wash over her. Her hands still in his, she let her body sway and gyrate to the music. She closed her eyes and let the music dictate her movements so she didn't see when Sean's eyes sent a silent signal to someone across the bar.

The band ended the song with a flourish of guitars and drums before picking out the melody to a slower song.

She opened her eyes and stared around her as the couples paired off and started slow dancing. Pulling her hand away from Sean, she started to turn to head back to the table when he grabbed her arm and pulled her close to him, almost slamming her into the front of him.

"Now, that's more like it," he said with a sneer.

"But I don't…" she started as she tried to pull her wrist out of his grasp.

"A marked woman here is fair game and I'm claiming my turn."

"But I'm not…" she started and then he wasn't there.

Her eyes widened when she turned and found Brock was holding the younger Wolf about two inches off the floor by his shirt collar.

"I didn't hear the lady agree," Brock growled.

She winced when Sean landed a blow to Brock's face. The other Wolf swung a fist and caught Brock in the face.

Two wolves stepped closer as they reached into their pockets, pulling out their weapons of choice, one had a wicked looking knife and the other a small pistol.

"I wouldn't," Brock said with a sneer as two of Harley's guards stepped forward, the badges of their job prominent on their collars.

"Brock, what are you doing here?" Mac hissed at him. "You're embarrassing me."

"Bonded Wolves don't frequent places like this unless they're looking for a hookup. If you weren't looking for a quick fuck you shouldn't have worn that shirt that shows off my mark."

She stared at him. Was he insinuating she was a slut? "Brock, I had no idea…"

"I know," he said as Sherry tried to back away. "You," he said as he pointed at Sherry, "will present yourself to court tomorrow morning. If you don't, I will personally come and find you."

Sherry nodded and backed into Cody who steadied her with his hands, his eyes narrowed at her. "You kept me occupied so this slimy piece of shit could get closer to Mac?"

"But, I didn't mean, he said he…"

"Yeah, I'm sure you didn't mean to put Mac in danger," Cody replied as he stepped back, his attention going to the Wolf Brock was glaring at. "And who are you? Did someone put you up to this?"

"No one put him up to it," Brock said with a sneer. "What brings you back to Red Tail territory, Sean? Gladieux find out what a piece of shit you are and throw you out?"

"Just slumming," Sean replied as he straightened his shirt.

"No, really, why are you here?" Brock asked as he stepped closer to Sean, Harley's guards standing ready.

Sean reached over and brushed at Mac's hair. "Gladieux wants his prize back. That she is yours just makes it even better."

Brock's nostrils flared as his hands tightened on Mac's arms. "Brock, what's he talking about?" She could feel the struggle between him and his Wolf as they wanted to shred some flesh.

"Why Sherry?" Brock asked.

"Anyone could see how she burned with jealousy over this pink haired slut. Convincing her to help me was easy." Sean crossed his arms and grinned at Brock.

"Yeah. He stopped me on my way to The Alpha's house this morning and gave me a bunch of money to make sure Mac was here tonight wearing something that showed off your mark," she mumbled at Brock with her head bowed.

"Dammit," he muttered as he grabbed Mac's hand. "Take him to The Beta," he growled at the guards.

Mac tried to pull her hand out of Brock's grasp. An angry Brock did not look like a fun time. "No. I want Cody to take me home."

His eyes went dark as night and he pulled her toward the door, his hand around her wrist like a manacle. "Until The Alpha says otherwise, you are my mate and will act accordingly. No mate of mine will be seen leaving a place like this with any other male wolves." His words came out rough, as if from deep inside him. Pulling her close to him he bent his neck and kissed her. Not some peck on the cheek kiss, a full-on, tongue down her throat kiss as his free hand pushed the small of her back so she was plastered to him.

When he ended the kiss, she stood there and stared at him. She knew how she felt about him but now, now it looked like those feelings might be mutual.

"Damn," he muttered as he pulled her toward the exit. "Your brother better make up his mind soon."

"Hey," she said as he dragged her across the parking lot. When he stopped and looked back at her glaring at him. "Slow down! I can't run in these heels."

"Oh, for fuck's sake," he growled and picked her up. "Hold on."

She snuggled into him, letting herself enjoy being close. A girl could definitely do worse than Brock Atkinson.

Brock

When he stopped and set Mac on her feet she looked around in confusion. "Where's your truck?"

"I didn't drive my truck." He walked up to a motorcycle and unlocked the left saddlebag. Pulling out a helmet, he handed it to her. "Put this on."

She tried to hand it back to him. "I don't want to get on that thing."

He took it from her hand and put it on her head, buckling the strap and adjusting it until it was snug. "Well, I'm not walking home," he said as he straddled the bike. He pointed to a peg, "Step there and swing your leg over."

"I don't want to…" she gulped, shaking her head.

"Why don't you want to ride on the back of my bike?"

"I know what that means, being on the back of a guy's bike."

He grinned at her. "You read one of those biker romances, didn't you? Well, that's only if you're in a club, besides, you've already got my mark on you. So, what's the real reason?"

He watched as she studied the toes of her shoes as she mumbled, "I don't want to be that close to you. You already broke the rules tonight and I don't want to…"

Now, instead of a chuckle he laughed. "What rules?"

"Harley told me to stay away from you until he decides about our mating. I don't want him to be mad at me."

"How about I make you a promise?" He stood in front of her and took her hand in his. "I promise to keep my hands to myself. I'm a grown man and I can control myself."

"You promise?"

"Yes, I promise to keep my hands to myself unless you initiate it."

"Okay then, let's go." She stood next to the bike. "You said it was this peg?"

He settled himself on the bike and pointed to the peg. "Yes, that one."

She hesitated slightly before she stepped up and swung her leg over the bike. Scooting as far back as the seat would let her, she looked for something to hold onto.

Brock reached behind him and pulled her closer. "You have to hold on to me or else you could fall off." He placed her hands at his waist and started the bike. "Lean into the turns like I do." And with a roar they were off.

Mac

With the first burst of speed, she plastered herself to Brock's back and held on tight, her eyes closed. Scents of pine trees and grass tickled her nose so she took a peek.

The world rushed by in a blur of colors. She felt more than heard Brock's chuckle.

She smiled, enjoying the warmth of his body. The wind rushing by was cool and she shivered making her wish she'd brought a jacket.

When he pulled up into the driveway of her brother's house she sat up, already missing the warmth of him. She rubbed her hands up and down her arms as he swung his leg over and dismounted.

He watched her shiver. "Shit, Mac, why didn't you let me know you were cold?" he shrugged off his leather jacket and dropped it onto her shoulders.

The scents of leather and male Wolf wafted up and she shivered again, but not because she was cold.

She stared at his face as he unbuckled the strap and pulled the helmet off her head, memorizing the curves of his cheekbones. *Sigh*.

When he smirked, she put her hands up and tried to

smooth down her hair. She hopped off the bike and bent over to look into the mirror, wincing at the tangled mess. Combing her fingers through her hair she looked up when he laughed.

"What's so funny?"

"You being all girly. As If I haven't seen you after three days in the woods." He stepped closer and focused his gaze on her mouth.

"What? Do I have something in my teeth?" She started to turn to look into the mirror again.

"No," he said as he rubbed his thumb over her bottom lip. "Fuck it," he declared softly before bending and taking her mouth with his. Even though it was softer than the kiss at Moonbeam, this kiss seemed to be more. More intense. More meaningful.

Her hands splayed against the fabric of his t-shirt, the thump of his heart spiking as his tongue teased hers.

She grabbed his shirt in her hands and sagged against him.

Reluctantly, he ended the kiss. Setting her back from him be brushed stray hairs behind her ear. "I shouldn't have done that."

She stared at him, her green eyes wide as she reached up to touch her lips. With a shake of her head, she stepped back, as if she was afraid to be too close to him.

"So, what's the story between you and that Wolf at the club?"

His face went hard and she instantly regretted bringing it up. "Never mind, it's none of my…"

"You deserve to know as it got you into something you didn't ask for." He ran his hand through his hair. "Back when your dad died, there was a vote on who would be the temporary Alpha until Harley was of age. Sean's dad had put his name in and was pissed when the vote went in favor of my dad. He'd always been jealous that my dad was The Beta and now he was going to be The Alpha. He blamed my dad when his dad couldn't handle getting beat. He got drunk and plowed his car into a tree."

"Oh, how awful."

"Yeah, after that he hated me and did everything he could to make my life hell. About a year ago he renounced his fealty to The Alpha and the Red Tail Pack and hooked up with Gladieux."

She reached up and brushed her fingers over the red mark on his cheek from the punch. "Does this hurt?"

"No, it'll be healed in an hour, don't worry about it."

She dropped her hand and stepped back. "Well, I… thanks for the ride." She turned toward the house and he grabbed her arm to stop her.

"I'm sorry. I shouldn't have kissed you like that, but I don't I regret it."

Pulling her arm out of his grip she fled to the front door, stopping short when it opened as she sped up the steps and into the waiting arms of her brother.

Rubbing his hands through his hair, he turned to walk into the house, sure Harley was going to rip into him for that kiss.

Chapter Twelve

Mac

Her brother's arms held her tight and she hugged him back. She was so confused.

She looked up at him. "Don't be mad at me."

"What happened? Are you okay?" Harley asked, his brow furrowed in concern.

"I'm okay."

Harley steered Mac toward the stairs. When Brock put his foot on the first step he turned and said, "You have your assignment."

Brock turned and stalked out of the house, slamming the door behind him.

Mac walked up the stairs and toward her room. At least, she hoped it was still her room. She'd gone against the one thing her brother had specifically told her not to do.

Plopping down onto her bed, she picked up Charleykins and held him to her chest, wishing the stuffed animal could take her place. Memories of irate foster parents flicked through her consciousness, making her tremble.

Harley noticed her shaking and hurried to pull her into a hug. "Hey, it's okay."

"But I made Brock break your rule."

"What rule? I just wanted to talk to you about Moonbeam and why you shouldn't be in places like that showing Brock's mark."

"Oh, never mind. Brock explained about places like that."

"Good," he replied as he set her away from him so she could return to her seat on the bed. "Now, what rule were you talking about? I don't remember giving Brock any rules."

She put her face into the top of Charleykins head and said, "Brock kissed me. I know he's supposed to stay away from me but…"

With a chuckle he interrupted her, "Hey, it's okay. I'm not going to punish you for kissing your mate. As Wolves, we're both territorial and passionate."

"You're not mad?"

He sat next to her on the bed and took her hand in his. "I don't know how you knew I told Brock to stay away from you but it wasn't that I didn't want you two together." He brushed at a tear rolling down her cheek. "I just wanted him to give you time to get used to the idea. That's all."

"But I thought you were mad because you hadn't approved the mating in advance."

"It's a custom, sure, but I only put a hold on things because of the way it happened. I wanted you to have a chance to make up your mind about it."

She pulled her hand out of his and wiped her cheeks. "I think I want to stay mated to Brock," she said as she looked at him hesitantly. "Is that okay?"

He smiled, a true smile that reached his eyes. "Of course it's okay. Brock has always been like a brother so…"

With a squeal she hugged him before she jumped up

hurried over to her dressing table and picked up her hairbrush and ran it through her hair. She bent over to look in the mirror.

"You've grown up," Harley commented.

She turned around. "What?"

"You've outgrown this room. With everything going on I forgot I promised you could redo it."

It had been nice to have something that felt familiar so she hadn't said anything about changing it. "Why bother? If our mating is approved, why would I need a room here? Shouldn't I be living with him? I mean, I think he wants this mating too."

"He told me that but I need you to continue living here for now. With you being on Gladieux's radar and the threats against Brock, the safest place for you is here. Besides, Brock just left on a special assignment for me."

"He left? Without saying goodbye?" She set the brush down. "Maybe he doesn't really want to be mated to me." She turned away from her brother so he wouldn't see the tears that threatened to spill down her cheeks.

Her brother pulled her into his arms and hugged her. "That's my fault. Believe me, he does want to be mated to you." He stroked her hair and continued, "Gladieux was sighted not far from here and I ordered Brock to go immediately. I'm sorry."

Chapter Thirteen

Mac

The edge of the step was hard against her back as she sat and stared into the empty coffee cup in her hands as if the answers to all the world's problems could be found there. After the spectacle she'd made of herself at Moonbeam, she'd stayed in the house for the last three days. She didn't want to make another oopsie that would look bad on her brothers. Her new furniture had been ordered and Cody had just finished painting the walls.

The roar of a motorcycle engine brought her attention to the road leading into their neighborhood. She didn't recognize the bike but her Wolf started howling. "Mate!"

Brock had returned from his special assignment. Mac stood and wiped her suddenly damp palms on her jeans. She didn't hear Harley walk into the room as her attention was on her mate. Brock brought the bike to a stop and swung his leg over as he turned the motor off.

"Brock!" she screeched, running toward him, jumping into his arms after he set the helmet on the seat.

She shoved her face into his neck and inhaled his unique scent as her Wolf practically vibrated with happiness.

"Hey, beautiful," he said before his lips found hers.

Harley cleared his throat loudly.

Brock blushed at being caught breaking etiquette in front of his Alpha. He set Mac on her feet in front of him. "Mac, you never greet another Wolf before your Alpha does."

"Huh?" she asked as she looked from Brock to Harley and back again.

"If you are in the presence of The Alpha, he will greet any Wolves first. It's a sign of respect for his title."

Mac turned around and looked down at the ground to hide the dismay on her face. "I'm sorry, Alpha. Please forgive my blunder."

"Mac," Harley said as he used his finger to pull her chin up. "It's okay. I didn't think about having someone teach you Wolf etiquette."

"You're not mad?"

"How could I be mad for something I didn't teach you?" He pulled her in for a brief hug. "Now that Brock's back he can teach you what you need to know."

She looked over at her mate. "I'm sorry…"

"Don't you tell me you're sorry for running up and jumping into my arms. Best homecoming I've ever had."

He nodded toward Harley. "I've got a lot to tell you." He turned back to Mac and took her hand in his. "I've got to take care of business first and then we can talk."

"Okay," she said as she watched the two Wolves go into the house.

Once they were out of sight she looked down at clothes. She'd thrown on her old jeans and a t-shirt not expecting Brock to come home. She couldn't remember if she'd even combed her hair that morning. Brock hadn't seemed to mind but she'd wanted to look nice when he returned.

Running into the house, she flew up the stairs and into her room, slamming the door behind her. She had to hurry. She didn't know how long their meeting would last and she wanted to look more like a woman than a bedraggled teen.

Brock

He stared at his Alpha, not quite believing what he'd just proposed. "A pack meeting tonight?" There went his plans to spend the evening with his mate. His Wolf growled in frustration.

"Yes, I have an announcement I think you'll want to hear sooner rather than later."

"Tell me now."

Harley laughed. "Nope, you've got to wait until tonight."

Brock folded his arms across his chest, his feet spread apart, showing his agitation.

"Go, I'm sure Mac is on pins and needles waiting for you."

"I'm surprised at how much I've missed her," he admitted as he rubbed at the tense muscles in the back of his neck.

"Be back here at five thirty for the meeting. Make sure Mac at least knows pack meeting etiquette."

At that he turned and waved his hand at his friend as he walked away. "Yeah, I'll do that."

Once he was out of the house, he hurried over to his bike and pulled his bag out of the saddlebag before heading next door to his childhood home. His mom would be glad to see him and he could tell her about what he'd found.

After a shower and dressed in clean jeans and a button-down shirt, he headed next door to give his mate a lesson in Wolf etiquette.

He stepped up onto the porch as the front door opened. Mac stood there in a dress and high-heeled boots, looking like the royalty she was. His Wolf chuffed a soft "*mine*" as he took her hand.

"My brothers are in the study getting ready for the pack meeting." She twirled in front of him. "Is this pack meeting appropriate?"

He wanted nothing more than to kiss her until she couldn't remember her name, but they had more important things to attend to.

"You look beautiful."

Her cheeks reddened as she took his hand and led him toward the staircase.

"We can't, or, I mean, we shouldn't be alone in your room." He pulled her closer to him and he brushed her hair behind her ear. "The Alpha hasn't officially sanctioned our mating so technically it isn't valid yet."

"Well, that's just stupid," she said and crossed her arms. "It's not hurting anyone."

"I know it's frustrating, but you are the pack princess so everything you do is going to be scrutinized."

She relaxed a bit. "But, how will anyone know if we spend time together alone in my room?"

"I'll know." He pulled her closer for a hug, kissing the top of her head. "Did you know that if Levi finds a mate outside of this pack, I'll be the obvious pick for Beta as my father was Beta for your father when he was The Alpha? That means my life, past and present, will be scrutinized by all the Wolves in the pack. Any hint of impropriety will reflect badly on The Alpha."

"Oh okay, I get it."

"Now, we can use the family room." He took her hand and led her to the back of the house. "Do you need something to drink before we get started?" he asked as he opened the fridge.

"No, I'm good for now."

He pulled out a beer and unscrewed the cap. "Well then, let's get started." He hoped he'd be able to get through everything he needed to tell her before he gave in to the urge to kiss her.

Mac

Mac stood to the left of her brothers in front of the row of chairs toward the back of the raised dais as the pack filed into the meeting room. She hoped her stomach wouldn't growl too loudly as the aromas from the attached kitchen wafted around the room, eliciting a few comments from the pack. The women had done well with the short notice.

She followed when Levi took her hand and motioned for her to sit next to him as Harley motioned for the pack to be seated.

Harley stepped to the front edge of the dais and looked out over his pack. "Thank you for coming. Sorry for the short notice but I couldn't call the meeting until Brock returned from his mission."

He explained how Brock had been dispatched to gather any intel he could find on Gladieux and his plans.

"It has come to my attention that young Wolves have gone missing over the last couple of months from a few surrounding packs. Brock was tasked with gathering information about these disappearances. We believe the kidnappings have all been done under the direction of Gladieux."

He stopped and took a drink of water before he continued.

"I am hoping for a peaceful resolution, but I need for everyone to be prepared if we need to go to war against the Black Paw Pack."

Several Wolves raised questions and Harley answered, giving his pack all the information Brock had gathered over the last few days.

Once everyone had settled back down, he stood tall.

"As you all know, our sister was recently returned to us after many years. We, my brother and I, and the entire pack owe an unpayable debt to Brock Atkinson for returning her to us."

He motioned for Brock to come up on the dais as he walked over to where Mac sat. He held out his hand , bringing her to where Brock stood.

"I'm sure the rumors have been flying about the unsanctioned mating between my sister and Brock. Today, I am declaring their mating true and binding."

Chapter Fourteen

Mac stood in front of the bathroom mirror, staring at her reflection. Now that their mating was official, she had doubts. Sure, he seemed attracted to her but what did she know?

She'd been surprised when her brother announced it at the pack meeting without warning her first. Her mind had been whirling with questions. Did Brock really want to be mated with her? Where would they live? She'd tried to ask Brock but he'd shushed her by kissing her. Well, that answered one of her questions anyway.

Then, he'd plopped her on the back of his motorcycle and they'd roared away from the meeting house toward the edge of town. He'd pulled into the driveway of a cute little cabin nestled on a wooded lot in an older neighborhood.

"Who lives here?" she'd asked as she undid the clasp on the helmet Brock had put on her.

Brock grinned. "We do. At least I hope we do." He took the helmet from her and grabbed her hand. "I mean, I own it. I hope you like it."

She pulled him toward the front door. "I love it!"

Once they were on the porch Brock unlocked the door but kept her from going through it. He set the helmet down on the porch and picked her up.

"What are you doing?"

"Isn't it traditional to carry the bride over the threshold?"

"But, today wasn't our mating day."

"So what?" He carried her into the living room and set her on her feet, kissing her when her feet touched the floor. "Take a look around while I go get some stuff from the bike."

She walked over to the couch and ran her hand along the back of it. The couch sat across from a huge fireplace with a television mounted above the mantle. A small dining table with four chairs sat to the right of the fireplace in front of a small kitchen area.

Brock returned and plopped a couple of bags on the floor near the hallway that probably led to the bedroom.

"How did you get my bag?" she asked when she realized she recognized the backpack.

"While you and I were going over pack meeting etiquette, Levi packed your bag for you."

"So, you knew?"

"That Harley was going to declare our mating true at the pack meeting? No." He picked up her backpack and slung it over his shoulder. "Though, I did suspect when I spied your brother trying to sneak out of the house with your bag."

"Are you happy about it?"

"The mating? Of course I am."

"Well, I mean, it did kinda happen by accident…"

He reached out and took her hand, pulling her down the hallway past a room set up with exercise equipment and a bathroom. "Best accident ever," he declared as he pulled her into the bedroom at the end of the hall.

He dropped the bags at the end of the bed and pulled her to him. Gently, he kissed her.

The too-brief kiss had her heart thumping crazily in her chest. "I, uh, I... could I have a couple of minutes?" she asked, staring at her shoes.

"Sure. Take your time."

At that she grabbed her backpack and hurried back to the bathroom, slamming the door behind her.

A soft knock on the door had her stomach plummeting to what felt like her feet. What if he said he liked her well enough but...?

"Coming," she called out as she tried to calm her racing heart. Just the thought of him rejecting her had her feeling like she wanted to puke Sure, he said he was happy but what if that was just to be mated to The Alpha's sister? Surely that would bring him some perks. *Deep breath, Mac,* she told herself as she wiped her suddenly sweaty palms on her pajama bottoms. *Geez, pajamas? Should she change into something sexier?*

Another soft knock on the door. "Mac, you okay?"

"Uh, yeah, be out in a sec." *A sec? Geez, could she sound any more like a kid?*

She forced herself to put her hand on the doorknob and turn it. Stepping into the hall, she could see Brock's back as he rummaged in a drawer of the dresser in the bedroom across the hall.

"Sorry I took so long."

Brock stood and turned to look at her, a pair of sweatpants in his hand. "I thought maybe you changed your mind."

"No, I just..." she stopped and took a deep breath. "I'm a little nervous. I mean, I don't know how to be someone's mate. And I'm sure I'll screw up again and I don't want anyone to think badly of you," she blurted out before she could lose her nerve.

He rubbed his hands up and down her arms. "I've never had a mate before so how about we figure that out together?" Hugging her close to him, he kissed the top of her head. "Now, do you want anything? Are you hungry? I noticed you picked at your dinner but you didn't seem to eat much of it."

"I was too nervous to eat," she admitted.

"Nervous about what?"

"You, me, us, everything." Hesitantly she brought her hands up to his shoulders. "I'm afraid I'll do something stupid and it will reflect badly on you and my brothers." She ran her hands down his arms. "But mostly I'm afraid you don't really want to be mated to me."

Suddenly, her front was plastered to his front.

"Can you feel that?"

She almost asked "feel what" but his lips found hers before she could speak her thought out loud. Now was not the time for snark.

As his lips moved against hers, she gave in to the call of his Wolf to hers and kissed him back as her hands searched for the button to his jeans. Her lady parts clenched at the memory of the last (and only) time they'd been intimate. He would be a full participant this time.

He moved her hands out of the way and took care of undoing his jeans before shoving them down his legs. As he stepped out of his jeans his hands went to the bottom of her top.

Her breath caught in her throat when she saw the way his eyes were blazing with need, looking almost black.

Brock

He hoped she didn't see how his fingers trembled when he pulled her top up and over her head, baring all of her to him.

She bit at her bottom lip and he almost lost control.

With a groan, he shucked his shirt and threw it to the side before slamming his lips on hers and kissing her again as his hands untied the drawstring on her pants. After they dropped to the floor his hands roamed up and down her sides, Gods, he wanted nothing more than to sink into her warm heat but he didn't want to scare her.

She inched her hips back and grabbed his hand, putting it between them at the apex of her thighs.

His fingers brushed against her nub and he felt her entire body clench with need. Swirling his fingers around that spot, he spread her wetness to prepare for what his Wolf was howling for.

He stepped back and picked her up, depositing her on the bed.

Taking a moment, he studied her, loving how her face was flushed and her lips puffy from his kisses. So beautiful and all his.

His Wolf growled with need as hers answered. Moving slowly, he kneeled over her, one hand on the bed near her head and the other on his cock, ready to sink into her and the welcome oblivion. He probed her entrance as she lifted her head and found one of his nipples with her tongue. That was all it took and he entered her in one swift movement, stopping when she gasped against his chest.

"Did I hurt you?"

"No, I just feel so… filled." She lowered her head back to the pillow and looked up at him. "Please," she implored him.

"Please, what?" he asked, not wanting to do anything to hurt her.

"Please move, it feels so... Aaaaah," she sighed as he pulled back and then pushed back into her.

His Wolf howled with glee when she began lifting her hips to bring him even deeper into her.

The tingle started at the base of his spine but he pushed it back, wanting to be sure she reached her own climax. He reached between them to let his fingers give her nub a few tweaks and he felt her walls begin to flutter against him.

That broke his control and he let himself go, his hips moving in unison with her as they both found their release.

His heart slowed as he nestled her in his arms and kissed the top of her head.

She looked up at him with a lazy smile. "I knew it would be better when you were fully conscious," she blurted.

He watched her cheeks go crimson before she shoved her face into his chest.

"Gah, can't believe I said that."

Just feeling her breath against his chest made him ready to go again. "You know, you can say anything with me."

She propped herself up on one elbow, her other arm reaching over to explore the dips his muscles made in his skin. "Do you remember the first time?"

"Some. I thought it was a fever dream until I felt the mating tattoo burning into my skin."

"I have another question but I'm afraid it will piss you off."

"Nothing you could ask me would piss me off right now. I don't think my Wolf has ever been this mellow," he said with a lopsided grin.

"Do you regret it? Us being mated, I mean."

"No. If I did, I would have petitioned your brother to declare our mating void."

"It's just that I'm so... awkward about the whole pack

thing. Wouldn't it be easier with someone who understands everything about pack life? I mean, I've already embarrassed you with my stunt at Moonbeam."

He reached over and brushed her hair behind her ear, his fingers tracing the curve of her cheek. "I was more angry that you grew up alone without your pack. You had no idea what you were doing would be frowned upon."

"I'm still sorry for that." She nestled into his arms and let her eyes close. Before long, her breathing deepened as she fell asleep.

He nuzzled her hair, breathing in her scent intermingled with the scent of their lovemaking. His Wolf sighed and he followed her into dreamland.

The scent of bacon and coffee tickled his nose as he woke. Stretching, he yawned as he looked to the other side of the bed. Panic momentarily took over until he heard her belting out a the lyrics to a classic rock song. He grinned at her slightly off-key rendition of Werewolves of London.

Pulling on the sweats he'd dropped on the floor, he settled them at his hips and rubbed his hands through his hair.

After a quick stop in the bathroom he sauntered into the kitchen, stopping at the coffee pot to fill a mug while he watched his mate swing her hips in time to the song playing through the Bluetooth speaker as she mixed eggs in a bowl.

He set the coffee mug on the counter and walked up behind her. Leaning forward he kissed her just behind her ear as his arm went around her waist and pulled her back into him.

The fork she'd been using to stir the eggs went flying as she jerked and pulled away from him.

"Mac, it's just me. It's okay."

Her body rigid, she stared up at him, her green eyes wide with fear. "Oh, God, I'm sorry, I…"

He silenced her with a quick kiss. "It's okay. Obviously that wasn't a good idea," he said as he ran his fingers through his hair. "I didn't mean to startle you."

Bending down to pick up the fork she replied. "Well, I don't like someone sneaking up on me."

"Obviously. But why?" he asked curiously.

"I don't want to talk about it."

"Did someone hurt you? Was it one of Gladieux's men?" he practically growled. "I'll take their head off." He turned and put both hands on the counter and lowered his head as he tried to get his Wolf under control. *"Someone put their hands on my mate?"*

When he turned back around, he found Mac standing in front of the sink with her arms wrapped around herself with tears running down her face.

"Mac, beautiful, it's okay."

Her lower lip trembled. "I made you mad," she whispered between sobs.

He pulled her into a hug, tucking her head into his chest. He felt each sob down to his soul. "Who hurt you? Did they take advantage of you?"

She went stiff in his arms. "Did they rape me? Is that what you're asking? You afraid you got yourself a tainted mate?"

"No, that's not what I asked." He rubbed at the suddenly tense muscles in the back of his neck. An innocent kiss had changed the scene of domestic bliss into one of fear and hurt.

She sagged against him. "I'm sorry, I just, I thought I was over it. I guess I'm not." She wrapped her arms around him and plastered herself to him.

He took her hand and led her to the couch. "Sit."

The fear crept back into her face. "You're getting all growly again."

He cleared his throat and tried again. "Please sit, we need to talk about this."

"It was long before I met you. Why do we need to…"

"Because whatever happened is still affecting you now. Talking about it is the only way to work through it."

Crossing her arms she stared up at him. "What if I don't want to talk about it?"

"Sorry, beautiful, but you're going to tell me. As your mate it is my right to punish anyone who has hurt you." He sat next to her and stroked her cheek with his thumb. "The thought of someone hurting you, my fated mate, is tearing a hole in my soul."

Her arms relaxed and she put her hands in her lap. "They probably thought I wanted…" she started.

With a low growl he interrupted. "Did you tell them no?"

"Of course I did," she blurted out.

"Well then, no matter if they were Wolf or human, they should have stopped. Tell me what happened."

She swiped at her bangs on her forehead nervously. "It was a couple of days after I ran away from the group home. Living on the street was still so new and scary to me I jumped at the chance when this cute guy told me he had somewhere I could stay."

Three years ago

Mac followed Rand through the park, hoping that the place he said was available was at least clean. She'd stayed away from the shelters, too many people in a small space made her Wolf edgy. Sleeping under the bridge had at least afforded some protection from the rain but with only a thin blanket it wasn't enough.

He led her through a hole in the fencing around what looked like an abandoned apartment building. A group of people were sitting on the steps smoking what smelled like weed. Her Wolf whined, *"Don't like this."*

"It will be okay," she reassured her Wolf even as she thought maybe this wasn't such a good idea.

Rand pushed open a door. "I know it's not much but it is warm and dry." He took her pack from her hand and set it in the corner next to a rolled-up blanket.

"He smells of deceit," her Wolf said as she continued to sniff the air.

"He's just being nice," Mac insisted, as she wondered why the good looking guy was helping her.

"There's a gas station on the corner with a fairly clean bathroom. Just be sure to go before dark, this neighborhood isn't the best."

"Why are you helping me?" Mac asked as she squatted to open her pack. She had some granola bars she'd found in the dumpster behind the grocery store. Maybe he wanted one.

"You look way too green to have been living on the streets very long. Finding a safe space to sleep is one of the first things you need to do."

"Well, thank you," she said as she held out one of the granola bars to him. "Are you hungry?"

"No, I'm good. You keep it." He brushed at something on his shirt. "Well, I've got to go. Do you think you'll be okay here by yourself? I could stay a little longer if you want me to."

With a blush she replied, "No, that's okay. Thanks for showing me this place."

"Glad to help." He walked out the door, pulling it closed behind him.

Now that she was alone her Wolf relaxed. "*Don't like him.*"

"*He was just trying to help.*"

Unrolling the blanket he'd left for her, she made a space to sleep. Pulling out the thin blanket she already had, she tried to get comfortable enough to fall asleep. She felt exposed even though she was inside a building.

She jolted awake as a hand stroked her cheek. When she tried to move someone draped themselves over her, keeping her pinned to the ground. "Let me up," she screamed before a hand covered her mouth.

"Shhh…, be quiet," a voice whispered in her ear. "We don't want anyone else joining the party, do we?"

Her eyes wide, she peered at the person holding her down. "Rand, what are you doing?"

"Taking what you owe me for finding you a place to sleep," he said as he leered at her, his hand pulling the front of her shirt up to expose her chest to him. "So pretty," he murmured as his hands went to her breasts.

"No!" she screamed as she bucked under him, her hands frantically pushing at his chest. No way was she going to let this happen. She should have left when her Wolf said she didn't like him.

With a snarl, her Wolf rushed forward giving her the strength to push him off of her.. Jumping to her feet, she brandished her claws at him.. "I suggest you leave now."

"What the fuck are you?" he asked as he scooted away from her.

"Just know that if you try this again with anyone else, I will find you and rip you to shreds."

He stood and ran out of the room.

Crumpling to the ground she hugged her knees up to her chest and rocked as her Wolf paced. *"Told you he was no good."*

The next day she headed out of town, she couldn't risk Rand finding her again.

Present Day

Brock's Wolf snarled. *"Fucker tried to hurt my MATE!"*

Mac placed her hand on Brock's cheek. "But he didn't. And I learned to not trust anyone on the road."

Brock kissed the top of her head. "Why did you trust me?"

"My Wolf trusted you so I just followed along. I'm learning to trust my Wolf's instincts over my own." She swiped at the tears drying on her cheeks. "Maybe now I'll quit dreaming about that night."

"Oh, sweeting, I will always keep you safe."

"You can't promise that. I know you'll try but…"

"Yes, I'll do everything in my power to keep you safe. Always."

Chapter Fifteen

Mac

Mac wandered around the house, picking up her book from the coffee table and setting it back down. After living on the streets for so long she wasn't used to having so much free time. She'd cleaned their little house every day, making sure everything was perfect but that only took up so much time. Having so much time to read was wonderful but she needed something to do that would use up some of her pent-up energy. Even her Wolf was getting grouchy.

After washing up the plate and knife she'd used for her lunch, she grabbed the keys off the hook by the door and hurried out the door to the truck before she changed her mind. Since she needed something to do and they needed all the warriors they could get for the impending battle with Gladieux she hoped her brother would agree to her training with the warriors. At least it would get her out of the house and it would also increase her ability to defend herself. She knew some of the female pack members were warriors and hoped that would sway her brother to let her train.

She parked the truck near the training field, hoping Brock wouldn't be angry she drove it without his permission. She sat and watched the warriors exercising, searching for the telltale red hair of her brothers.

A knock on the window made her jump.

"Sweeting, what are you doing here?' Brock asked.

"I, uh, I wondered if Harley would let me train with the warriors. I'm bored and I want to do something useful." She rubbed her hands together nervously.

He opened the door and held out his hand. "Well, come on then."

Curious, she looked up at him as she slid to the ground. "You're not mad?"

"Why would I be mad?" he asked as he tucked her under his arm and steered her toward the practice field.

"I took your truck without asking and…"

He kissed the top of her head. "I was letting you get settled into life with a mate. I want nothing more than for you to be happy. So, what have you decided to do? Do you want to get a job, go back to school?"

She took a deep breath and blurted, "I want to train to be a warrior." Going back to school hadn't crossed her mind but maybe she could do that if they wouldn't let her train.

"That's a good idea. Not that I want you fighting in a battle," he clarified, "but training is a good use of your time."

"You're really not mad?" she asked as she watched Harley walk toward them.

He smiled. "No, I'm not mad."

"Hey Mac, what brings you by today?" Harley asked.

"It seems my mate wants to train to be a warrior," Brock said with pride in his voice.

"You know you don't have to…" Harley began.

"I know. I'm not used to being idle and I want to do something helpful."

"Okay then, if you're sure." He turned and motioned to Levi who was nearby. "We can always use another warrior."

Levi trotted up. "Yes, Alpha?"

"Our sister wants to train as a warrior. Please get her started and set her up with a training partner."

"Thank you, Harley!" she squealed as she turned toward her mate. "Are you sure you're good with this?"

"Of course, sweeting." He pulled her close for a kiss, stepping back with a grin when Harley cleared his throat. "Go, train."

She followed Levi to the group of warriors to learn her first lesson.

Three hours later, Mac sat on the ground and caught her breath from that last set of exercises. At first, she'd felt self-conscious being trained with the younger Wolves but as she'd followed along she realized she had a lot to learn about being a warrior. It wasn't just about strength, it was also about being smart and having the stamina to fight. She'd learned that not all Weres could transform on the fly. It was rare a rare skill that many tried to learn.

"So, how was your first day?" Brock asked as he dropped to sit next to her. "Make sure you stay hydrated," he said as he handed her a bottle of water.

"It was wonderful," she gushed. "At first I felt silly training with the kids but I realize I have a lot to learn. Did you know I can transform without even thinking about it?"

"I wondered. I know it's prevalent in your family. Actually," he said as she scooched closer to her, "I can do it too. It took me years of practice before I could do it."

"I imagine that's helpful in a battle."

"It is." He chugged from his own bottle of water. "Harley invited us over for dinner tonight unless you're too tired from training."

"That sounds nice. I should be okay after I have a shower."

Brock stood and helped her up, pulling her into his arms for a kiss.

Her brain went fuzzy and her knees threatened to buckle from the need swirling in her blood.

Brock ended the kiss and just held her for a moment before he backed away. "I'll meet you back at the house."

She nodded as her hand went up to her lips, amazed at how a kiss could stir up such need within her so quickly. Thoughts of continuing the kiss in the privacy of their home had her skipping toward the truck, ignoring the knowing looks from her brothers.

Brock's bike was in the drive when she pulled up to the house. She slid out of the truck and wished she didn't smell like she'd been training all day. As she walked through the living room, she heard Brock rummaging around in the fridge, probably looking to see if they had any beer left. "I'm hopping in the shower first," she yelled as she ran for the bathroom, dropping her clothes in a trail behind her. Turning on the tap she combed the tangles out of her hair as she waited for the water to get hot.

She'd just stepped into the shower and was wetting her hair when she heard Brock say, "Make room for me." The curtain opened and he stepped into the shower with her. He let out a groan when the hot water hit his back.

"You're hogging all the water," she said as she poured shampoo into her hand.

"Here, let me." He scraped the shampoo into his palm and moved her into the spray before his hands went to her hair. As he massaged the shampoo into her hair, Mac moaned. The gentle pressure of his fingers against her scalp sent tingles through her body. Who knew someone shampooing your hair could feel so good? His thumbs worked the muscles at the back of her neck and she placed her hands on the wall to hold herself upright. The suds from the shampoo raced down her body, leaving a slick trail for Brock's hands to follow.

After having her rinse the suds from her hair, he turned her around to face him, his hands going to her hips as he kissed her. The kiss deepened and one hand went to the back of her head and the other went up to caress her breast, tweaking the nipple until her legs threatened to give out. "Brock, ah, I…" as his lips kissed their way down to her neck.

Her hands wanted to caress him everywhere at once, and she tried.

They finally stepped out of the shower when the water started to cool. After wrapping a towel around his waist Brock used another to dry Mac. She shivered as his hands rubbed the warm towel across her skin. When his hands brought the towel up to her chest, she caught his hands in hers. "I think I better take it from here if we want to be on time."

"But this is so much fun," he said with a grin.

"Maybe you want to explain to my brothers, The Alpha and The Beta why we were late to a family dinner."

"Okay, okay. He let her have the towel, whipping his towel from around his waist to rub at his hair.

"No fair," she said as her Wolf begged to run her paws down his body to his penis that jutted out toward her. Standing on her tiptoes she kissed him without touching him and he growled, his hands going to her waist. "Stop it, we're going to be late," she said with a laugh as he held her from exiting the bathroom.

"Seriously, you realize I love you, don't you?" he said as he looked into her eyes.

Her cheeks pinked. "And I love you," she admitted as she stared down at her feet, feeling shy. Gathering her courage, she looked up at him. "Now, I need to get dressed," she said as she slid past him and out the door.

Seriously, he sure made it hard for her to resist him. Just a few weeks ago she'd been a captive and now she was mated. Sending up a silent thank you to the gods, she headed for the closet.

Brock

He absently finished drying off as he watched Mac saunter out of the bathroom. His Wolf growled softly, desire heating his blood.

"Calm down, we don't have time for another round right now."

His Wolf backed down with a whine.

Mac

Mac scooted closer to Brock until her leg touched his. Being mated was still so new to her and she cherished the alone time with him even though it was only a ten minute drive to her brother's. Once he stopped and parked in front of the house he turned to her and kissed her.

As they walked up the sidewalk, he took her hand in his, claiming her in that small way, showing everyone she was his.

"Should I knock?" she asked. "I mean it was my home but now it's not."

"I'm sure your brother expects you to just walk in, this will always be your home."

Her hand on the doorknob, she let out a squeak when it turned under her hand and the door opened. She looked up into the face of her brother, Levi.

"Mac, come on in. We're having drinks out on the deck. Help yourself. " He walked through the door and out onto the porch. "I've got to take this call," he said with a frown.

Mac watched as he hurried to his car. "I wonder what that's all about?"

They walked through the house to the sliding glass door leading out to the deck to find Harley deep in conversation with a beautiful brunette.

"Anya, this is my sister, McKayla Brock you already know…" He motioned toward Mac and Brock. "Mac, this is Anya, my girlfriend."

"Very nice to meet you, Mac. We were all so glad to hear you had been returned to us after all these years."

With a blush, Mac mumbled, "Thank you," not really knowing how to respond as her Wolf chuffed.

"She's only after position," her Wolf commented with a sneer in her voice.

"I'm sure Harley knows that. Now hush."

Harley reached down into the cooler next to his chair and pulled out a beer and handed it to Brock. "What do you want to drink, Mac? We've got beer, water, and I think there's some sodas in the fridge in the kitchen."

"Water is good for me."

After he grabbed a water from the cooler and handed it to Mac, Harley returned to his seat. "So, Mac, how did you like your first day of training?"

"I loved it! It felt so good to be doing something worth-while. I'm going to be so sore tomorrow, but it was so worth it."

Levi returned to the deck, mumbling about stupid females.

"Levi, what was that call about?" Harley asked.

Levi took a swig of beer before answering. "Some female from White Paw who says Gladieux kidnapped her son. She kept trying to tell me she was the Alpha. Personally, I think she's delusional, I'm not even sure she has a son."

"Do you want me to…" Harley asked as he reached for his phone.

"No, I've got it handled."

"Okay then." Harley stood. "So, who's ready for dinner?"

Chapter Sixteen

Mac

She slunk down the stairs hoping to avoid her brothers. It had been a week since Brock had left on another special assignment and she missed him. With everything going on with Gladieux, Brock didn't want her staying at their house alone so she was back in her room at her brothers' house. At least now it had been redecorated so she felt more comfortable. Her brothers and her mate meant well but they were just a bit over-protective, wanting to know where she was every minute of the day. It was wearing on her. At least she had her daily training to look forward to. But it wasn't enough, she needed a run through the woods before her Wolf got any more stir crazy.

Not wanting to take Brock's truck, she'd called Cody and asked him to meet her a block away. Her brothers would notice if the truck was gone and she really wanted to get away for just an hour or so. She snuck down the stairs, stopping when the last to the bottom step let out a loud creak. When neither brother appeared, she slowly opened the front door and slipped through, closing it silently behind her before hurrying down the sidewalk.

Cody was waiting in his truck just like she'd asked. He was still the only real friend she'd made since she'd come home to her pack. He turned to look at her when she opened the passenger door.

"Hey, Mac. Why did you have me park…"

"Never mind," she interrupted him. "I just needed a little time away from my brothers. I know they're only trying to protect me but I can take care of myself. I mean, I did it for years plus I have been training as a warrior."

"I get it," he agreed as he started the truck. "But, are you sure it's safe? There's been talk about Gladieux and how he disappeared a week ago."

"I know, that's why I'm back at my brother's while Brock is away. I swear, it's okay. I'll make sure you don't get in any trouble for this. A short run in the woods and I'll go back to the house, I promise." Her Wolf grumbled, looking forward to a run but not liking how Mac was sneaking out.

Cody put the truck in gear and pulled away from the curb, turning left toward the woods on the outskirts of town. Pack runs were always on the weekends so the woods should be empty.

Once Cody had parked in the meadow, Mac flung open the door and hopped down to the grass as she took a long sniff. "Aaah," she breathed as she took in the scents of the forest. "Thank you," she said as she walked up to Cody and kissed his cheek, not noticing how his cheeks pinked at her attention.

Once she was in the trees, she stripped and folded her clothes, placing them under a large pine tree where she'd be able to find them again after she finished her run.

Ready for the exhilaration of a run, she looked over her

shoulder and grinned as Cody kicked off his shoes and unbuttoned his shirt.

"Come on, slowpoke!" she jeered as she fixed her route in her mind. "Last one to the lake's a rotten egg." Shifting to her wolf form mid-stride, she took off through the trees, her mind on how the cool water would feel against her bare skin before her Wolf fully took over.

Cody

He stood at the edge of the lake in Wolf form, his nose sniffing for the unique scent of Mac. He'd been right behind her, why wasn't she here?

The lake was undisturbed except by the slight breeze forcing small ripples across the expanse of water.

Brock

The breeze blowing in the window ruffled his hair as he sped down the highway. It had been a week and he needed to see his Mac. His Wolf growled at the thought of his mate.

"Relax," he muttered, "we'll be there in an hour." His wrist on top of the steering wheel, he looked relaxed but he was anything but. A week without being near his fated mate had him itchy and unfocused. He'd just finished filling up the gas tank when the pain hit, sharp and hot, in his chest. And then nothing. His Wolf whined, *"Mate?"*

That connection he'd had with Mac was gone as if it had never existed. Forcing himself to calmly return to the seat of his truck took all his concentration, his Wolf wanted to shift and howl. His hands shaking, he selected Harley's number on his phone's video call app.

When he saw his friend's face he blurted, "She's gone."

"Who's gone?" Harley asked, concern marring his features.

"Mac is gone. Our mate bond is gone."

He watched Harley turn and talk to Levi. "She should be up in her room getting ready for dinner. Levi's going…" He stopped when he heard a howl. "Shit."

Brock started his truck and ground out, "I'll be there in an hour. Find her!"

He ended the call and threw the phone on the passenger seat as he stomped on the gas and pulled out onto the highway. He didn't care that he'd just given his Alpha an order. Mac was his.

Harley

He stared at his phone in shock. Brock had just given him, The Alpha, an order. They'd be having a discussion about that after they found Mac. She'd slipped out and no one knew where she was. And he didn't like that the mate bond she had with Brock seemed to be gone.

His phone buzzed in his hand. Why would Cody be calling him directly?

"What?" he growled as he hurried out of his office and motioned to Levi.

He frowned as Cody relayed his story, that he'd brought Mac out to the woods for a run and how she'd disappeared without a trace.

Mac

She opened her eyes and squinted at the bright light in her eyes.

"She's coming around," a voice to her left said as she blinked, trying to focus.

"So, you thought you could get away," another voice said, a voice she remembered.

She tried to bring her hand up to wipe at her eyes and discovered her wrists were bound behind her back. At least this time the ropes weren't burning into her flesh. "You're going to regret this," she said through clenched teeth.

"Oh yes, you're much more valuable to me this time now that we know who you really are." He leered at her and her stomach dropped. "I'll have The Alpha right where I want him."

A prick on her arm and darkness overtook her.

Her eyelids felt glued shut when she tried to blink away the blackness. Willing her eyes open was taking all of her concentration. How long had she been out?

"It's okay."

Her eyes finally started to cooperate and she could open them to slits. The voice came again from her left as she felt a touch on her arm.

"You're okay for now."

The white blob next to her came into focus. Ice blue eyes beneath pure white bangs looked at her. Her Wolf grumbled sleepily.

She sat up and looked around the room. The cot beneath her was hard and smelled musty. She rotated her neck and heard it pop as the tendons and muscles stretched. "How long was I out?"

"Quite a while. At least a couple of hours."

She looked down and saw she was dressed in a dirty looking shapeless top and drawstring-waisted pants. Looking up, she scanned the room. The room looked similar to the one she'd been held in before with the exception of the high window in the corner covered in bars. There was sink along the back wall with a bucket beside it. She was back in Ankton in the basement beneath the auditorium.

She could feel her Wolf awakening as whatever drug they'd injected her with started to wear off, Rubbing at her wrists she appreciated that at least they hadn't used the wolfsbane this time. The screech of rusty hinges brought their attention to the door as it swung open. Three of Gladieux's men stepped in, one holding a gun and the other two holding a coil of rope and a leather collar with a leash attached. Mac shuddered at the memory of standing on display and being led around like a dog. She felt for the reassurance of her mate bond with Brock and was shocked when she couldn't find it at first. What did that mean? *Did that mean something had happened to Brock?* Then she felt the bond, muted and barely there.

Her Wolf howled in frustration.

She shook her head and backed away until her back hit the wall. The man with the rope made a move toward her and she had to concentrate to let her wolf out just enough to elongate her fingernails into claws as the guy with the gun laughed. "I wouldn't do that if I were you. wolfsbane coated bullets," he said with a sneer as he motioned at her with the pistol.

She forced her Wolf back, promising they'd get out of this and take that guy's head off when they did.

"Don't worry, princess, it's not your turn yet."

She watched in horror as they placed the collar on the other woman and she heard her hiss in pain as the wolfsbane soaked leather settled onto the bare skin of her neck. The memory of the burning made her want to curl up in a ball but she stood tall, watching as they led the woman out the door, the guy with the gun pointing it at Mac the whole time as if they feared her.

Once the door closed behind them, she returned to the cot and sat down, her knees weak. What the hell had they given her? They'd only been here a few minutes while they fitted the other woman with the collar but it felt like she'd been running for hours.

Her Wolf whined and she focused on trying to find the mate bond she had with Brock. Maybe she could somehow let him know where she was. The connection was faint but she couldn't feel his emotions like she normally could. That was weird.

About an hour later the door opened and they shoved the woman into the room and removed the collar. Once the door slammed behind them, Mac hurried to the woman and helped her over to the other cot. The skin of her neck was red and oozy.

She went to the sink and discovered some fairly clean cloths folded neatly on a shelf above it. That would have to do. Wetting one of the cloths with cool water she returned to the woman and placed the cloth on the worst of the oozy spots. "I don't know if this will help," she said, wishing for some of the salve Brock had used on her. "I'm Mac," she said as she blotted at the irritated skin with the cloth. "McKayla Jensen, er, Atkinson."

The woman looked up at her. "I've heard about you. You're The Alpha's sister, aren't you? I'm Pepper." She winced as Mac placed another cool cloth on her reddened skin. "Your brother is an asshole."

"Which one?" She asked as she sat on the cot next to her.

"Levi. I've talked to him on the phone a couple of times and he was just so rude and obnoxious to me."

"Wow, that doesn't sound like Levi at all. Are you sure it was him?"

"Yeah, I'm sure. If he'd listened to me, I wouldn't be in this mess."

"I know why I'm here, I'm leverage against my brother. Why are *you* here?"

Pepper brushed at a tear. "Gladieux thinks I'm going to mate with him." She sat up straight and brushed the hair out of her face. "I'm The Alpha of the White Paw Pack and I will not be forced to mate with some mangy, power-hungry, wanna-be, Wolf."

Puzzled, Mac asked, "You're an Alpha? I thought Alphas were male?"

"Generally, yes, that's true. But, for some reason I was born an Alpha. According to Wolf legends it used to be common for women to be Alpha's but as the packs dwindled, females needed to focus more on continuing the pack bloodlines."

"Oh," Mac said. "I haven't learned about that yet."

"Most packs ignore the old tales about female Alphas, the males like the balance of power being in their favor."

"So, your pack will be looking for you too. We just need to stay safe until someone finds us. She hoped Brock had noticed the absence of her emotions through their mate bond. At least Cody knew she was missing by now. She hoped her brothers wouldn't punish him too severely for him driving her out to the forest for a run. She'd known Gladieux's men were around but she thought she knew better than her brothers and she'd be safe because it was pack land. Mad at herself, she vowed to listen to them next time. If there was a next time.

Pepper stood and paced the length of the room and back. "My kidnapping will start a war between the packs unless we can get away before they attack." She paced some more.

"Hopefully my Beta had better luck when he contacted your brother for help after I disappeared."

Mac nudged at the mate connection, hoping whatever they'd dosed her with would wear off enough that she could feel the reassuring presence of Brock. Her Wolf was restless without the connection. She concentrated harder, giving up when the trying gave her a headache.

Pepper leaned back against the pillows and ran her hands through her bangs, tugging at them. She glanced at the window and said, "it's late, we should try to get some sleep. Gladieux won't do anything until morning."

"I don't think I'll be able to sleep."

"Try, we must be ready when a chance to flee presents itself. Gladieux isn't stupid but some of his thugs aren't very bright."

"Okay," Mac said as she leaned back and closed her eyes, willing the thoughts of what Gladieux would do in the morning away. Instead, she focused on thoughts of Brock. How he'd looked so handsome and strong when they'd faced Gladieux together and then how he'd looked when he let the worry creep into his features as he'd tended to her burned skin. And then, thoughts of the nights they'd spent together since their mating. She smiled as she drifted to sleep.

"Mac," Pepper hissed. "Wake up."

Propping herself up on her elbows she pried her eyes open and squinted at the other female. "What's going on?" she asked as she noticed the sun beaming in through the window.

Pepper stood and peered through the small window at the top of the door. On her tiptoes, she couldn't see much other than the tops of heads. "Something's going on, they're all running around and yelling at each other."

Mac jumped up and ran her hands through her hair, wishing for a hairbrush. "Can you tell what they're saying?"

Pepper stood with her ear to the window. "One guy just said something about The Alpha's men surrounding the auditorium. Sounds like your brothers are here to save you."

A key turned in the lock on the door. Mac jumped up and hurried over to stand beside Pepper, wishing she had some kind of weapon. Letting her Wolf out a bit, she felt the familiar ache as her fingers grew in length and her fingernails sharpened to deadly points. She was surprised at how much effort it took. Usually letting her Wolf out was easy but now, whatever they've dosed her with had muted the connection between her and her Wolf.

As the door swung open, they both tensed as the Wolf walked into the cell.

Pepper jumped first and raked her claws down his back as Mac swiped at his stomach. She felt her claws rip through skin and muscle, the thought of the damage she was doing to him making her feel a little nauseous. He swiped back at her and she jumped back, getting a good look at his face. He was the one who'd led her around in the leather collar and leash the last time she was here. With a growl, she let her Wolf take over, jumping toward him, her teeth sinking into the flesh of his neck, ripping out a huge chunk as he slumped to the floor. As she returned to her human form she heard Pepper mutter, "You're a vicious one, aren't you?"

"Fucker led me around on a leash. He got what he deserved." She picked up the clothes and frowned as the tunic had come apart at some of the seams when she'd shifted. Tying the tunic around her she pulled the pants up and tied the drawstring around her waist. "Shit, wish I would have stripped before I shifted."

They heard fighting out in the hallway, the sounds fading

as the fight moved away from them. Pepper grinned, "Looks like that's our cue to get gone. Come on, Mac, I'm sure someone will be around to check on us soon."

"Come on, this way," Mac said as she tugged on Pepper's hand as they ran past the double doors that opened to the auditorium. She remembered seeing a door with an exit sign above it down at the end of the hall. They needed to get out of the building.

As they ran, Mac stumbled when an intense feeling of grief came over the mate-bond, almost bringing her to her knees. She could feel Brock's Wolf howling in grief, the intensity of the grief overriding whatever they'd given her to mute their bond.

"What's wrong?" Pepper asked as she stopped and tugged on Mac's hand. "We've got to get…"

"Something's happened. My mate is grieving for someone very close to him. I've got to get to him." She pulled her hand out of Pepper's and took off back the way they'd come.

Blindly, she ran toward her mate, the feelings coming through the mate-bond making her want to stop and curl into a ball. Grief and anger mingled together, creating a blast of emotion that felt like it would blow the top off her head off if she let it.

"*Mate, grief,*" her Wolf whined as she stopped in the doorway to the auditorium.

She watched as Brock looked up at the ceiling and howled, the haunted sound raising gooseflesh on her arms.

"Brock! Behind you!" she screamed when she saw two of Gladieux's mean sneaking up behind his back.

He turned and shifted, swiping deadly claws into first one man and then the other, watching dispassionately as they dropped to the floor.

He shifted back, his hands and forearms covered in bloody gore.

"Mac," he growled as he stalked toward her. "Are you okay?" he asked as he ran his hands up and down her body, looking for injuries.

"I'm okay," she said as she tried to look around him toward the body he'd been kneeling in front of.

"Don't look, sweeting," he said as he pulled her into his arms and tried to move her back toward the door. "You don't want to see."

"Who is it? Is it Harley?" At the shake of his head she knew it was her other brother. "Levi?" she asked in a whisper.

"I'm sorry sweeting," he said gruffly, his voice thick with grief.

She struggled out of his embrace and ran to the body of her brother. "Oh, Levi," she wailed. She dropped to her knees. Tears flooded her eyes and she almost missed when Levi's hand inched toward her.

"Mac," he whispered, his voice weak with pain as his hand grabbed her arm weakly. "Tell Harley I…"

"Shhh…" she whispered as she brushed the blood matted hair off his head. "Don't try to talk. Save your strength to shift." She might be ignorant of most things Werewolf but even she knew their wolf form healed much faster than their human one. Something about the magical nature of their dual nature made it so.

She watched as his skin rippled but did not become fur covered.

"Can't," he panted before his eyes rolled back in his head.

Harley strode into the room, Pepper behind him. Surveying the room, he stopped when he saw Mac on her knees before the body of their brother, Brock beside her.

She heard his breath catch in his throat. "Levi? No!" he cried in a strangled voice.

Mac looked up at him. "He's still alive. I don't know how but he is."

Pepper stepped forward as Harley's men closed and blocked the doors to the room as Gladieux's men tried to gain entry. She pushed Harley out of her way as she hurried to Levi.

She dropped to Levi's side and peered at his wounds. "I need something to use as a bandage," she said as she held her hand out.

Brock picked up the remnants his shirt and handed it to her.

"Please help him," Mac cried as she rocked back and forth.

Pepper worked swiftly, binding up the worst wounds as best she could. "He needs proper medical care."

They heard chanting coming from outside the auditorium, chants of "The Beta is dead, The Alpha is next."

Harley looked into Pepper's eyes. "Can you save him?"

"I believe so, as long as we get him to my pack quickly."

He motioned to a couple of his men. "Take my brother wherever she says. Do not let anyone know Levi still lives."

They hurried to do their Alpha's bidding.

Mac stood and watched as Pepper directed their efforts.

"Can you really save him?" she asked worriedly.

"With some luck, yes. But I have to get him to my healers quickly." She hugged Mac and stepped back, her mind back on saving The Beta.

"But what about your son?"

Pepper turned back to her. "I can only hope Gladieux will realize he has more bargaining power with my son alive."

After checking the area outside the emergency exit, they

moved Levi toward the door. Before they moved out of the room they turned and gave a slight bow to Harley. "We'll get your brother to the White Paw Pack healers as quickly as possible," the senior Wolf said before turning and following his warriors through the door.

Harley stood and schooled his features. "You are all sworn to secrecy," he said as he looked from one face to another. "We are grieving for our Beta." He looked down at a dead Wolf near where Levi had been laying. After kneeling next to the body he picked up the remnants of Levi's shirt and draped it over the dead Wolf's face.

His remaining Wolves took up posts in a circle around him as Mac and Brock joined him next to the body. He put his head back and howled with grief as a few of Gladieux's men crept into the room, Gladieux himself striding in behind them.

Mac watched as Harley stood and glared at the pompous man standing before him.

"My brother is dead. You will pay for his death." He turned back and knelt to pick up the dead Wolf. "Present yourself to my pack in one week. If you do not, you will be hunted and killed like the coward I know you to be."

As Harley strode out of the room, Brock pulled Mac to his side and followed.

Chapter Seventeen

Mac sat at the table where just days before there'd been laughter and love but now, the mood had turned dark.

"Do you think he'll be okay?" Mac asked to no one in particular, her hands wrapped around a cup of coffee.

Brock pulled out the chair next to her and sat, pulling her left hand into his. "I hope so, Sweeting. White Paw is known for the skill of their healers."

She curled into her mate and took comfort from his arms around her. Her thoughts turned to her role and what happened.

"Harley, I'm sorry," she said as she peeked around Brock's arm at her brother. She felt it deep in her soul when he didn't even turn to look at her. "It's all my fault."

"How is it your fault, little sister?" he muttered as he stared at the coffee in the mug in his hands.

"How is it not?" She angrily swiped at a tear that ran down her cheek. "I'm the one who took off after you told me to stay put. If I hadn't gone for a run none of this would have happened."

Brock kissed her forehead and hugged her tighter. "Sweeting…"

He was interrupted as Harley stood. "I don't want to ever hear you blaming yourself for Levi's injuries. We all stormed Gladieux's stronghold knowing we might be hurt or even killed in the battle. This battle would have happened eventually."

"But it might have ended differently…"

"Yeah, our brother could be dead." He paced the length of the table and turned to pace back. "None of us know what the Gods have in mind for us." He stopped and stood in front of Mac, taking her hands into his. "If you have to blame someone blame Gladieux for forcing the situation."

Harley turned at a knock on the door.

"Enter."

The Wolf stopped just inside the door and bowed his head in deference to The Alpha. "I bring a message from the Alpha of the White Paw Pack."

"Continue," Harley almost shouted.

"The patient still lives. My Alpha inquires as to the timing for a rescue effort of her son who is being held by Gladieux."

With a frown Harley replied. "I am considering our options."

"She also asked me to relay an update on the other Wolves who are receiving medical treatment by her healers. All are healing well and should be back to full-strength within the next day or two as long as they obey the healer's instructions."

Harley barked out a laugh. "Thank you." He rubbed the unshaven whiskers on his chin as he considered his response. "Tell her her presence is required tomorrow at the memorial service. I'll be in touch soon with our plans regarding Gladieux."

After the door closed behind the retreating messenger Harley dropped down into his chair. "Jesus, that's good news. Now, we still need to put on a funeral worthy of The Beta tomorrow. Send out the announcement to the surrounding packs. Most of the Alphas and Betas are already here but protocol demands a formal announcement."

Brock stood and placed Mac in the chair. "I've got to help your brother with the arrangements for the memorial." He pulled her up and plastered her to his front as he kissed her.

Her face flamed red when she remembered her brother was in the room. "Brock, I don't think Harley wants to watch that."

He laughed as he winked at Harley. "I think he'll let it go this one time. Now, I want, no, I *need* you to stay here. Maybe you can go take a nap in your room?"

"A nap? Really? You do remember I'm not five, don't you?"

He leaned his head down toward hers and whispered, "Believe me, sweeting, I not going to forget."

Her cheeks flamed red again when her brother snorted. But, instead of bowing her head she grinned at him. "You better not! Now, I've got to go plan an appropriate mourning outfit for tomorrow." She stood on her tiptoes and planted a kiss on Brock's lips. "Go, do what you've got to do. I'll be waiting."

To be continued in Book 2, *Rise Of The White.*

About the Author

Romance author, dialysis warrior, furkid mom, and Best Fiends addict. Lover of coffee, 80's music, and all things romance. During the day she carves out writing time in between trips to the back door as doorman to her four-legged furry child. At night after spending quality time with her husband she chips away at her never-ending TBR pile.

Keep up with Hoosiergirl Publishing here:
https://hoosiergirl-publishing.kit.com/df28902ff9

You can find all her links on her website:
https://www.laremenicky.com

Also by RAGAN CARMICHAEL

https://www.lavishpublishing.com/authors/l-a-remenicky/

Saving Cassie (Fairfield Corners Book 1) - Everyone has secrets. Sometimes secrets can get you killed. After ten years in the big city, Cassie Holt is moving back to her hometown to take over the bookstore left to her by her beloved Gram, vowing to live her life alone. To her best friend, Sheriff James Marsten, Cassie seems to be the same girl that left Fairfield Corners to go to college but Cassie has secrets and one of those secrets could get her killed. When one of her secrets becomes a threat to her life, James turns to his new deputy to help him keep Cassie safe. Deputy Logan Miller has been burned by love and is not looking to get involved with anyone anytime soon. When he is thrown into close quarters with Cassie, the sparks begin to fly and he begins to see through the walls Cassie has built around her heart. As the threat gets closer, can Logan protect Cassie and protect his heart? (Mature Adult, 18+)

Ragan's Song (Fairfield Corners Book 2) - It only took one look into his eyes for Ragan to know she was in trouble. Adam Bricklin has heard the melody in his head for years, the melody that told him if a decision was right or wrong. When he met Ragan Newlin, the song told him she was the one. Devastated when circumstances tore them apart, it has taken three years for him to finally move past the heartbreak. With a new girlfriend, a new album in the works, and his daughter doing well in school, things are looking bright; until the day Ragan returned to Fairfield Corners bearing secrets that could change their lives forever. (Mature, 18+)

Loving Jessie's Girl - Fiercely independent, Rina Abbot hid her true situation from everyone, including her best friend, Jessie. Out of money and unable to care for her rescue dogs she had no choice but to accept the help of the handsome stranger with a familiar face. Afraid to trust him, she tried to ignore the feelings he stirred within her as they searched for his missing brother...

Preacher's Redemption - With the past and the present on a collision course can their love survive?

2nd Chance Valentine - A chance encounter in a bar with the one who got away had Cam Beckett dreaming of his own happily ever after. But, only if he could convince Kara to forget their disastrous first date and give him a second chance.

My Grumpy Valentine - Ashley Sweet was living her dream—baking cupcakes and making plans to expand her bakery—until Thorton Hodges walked in with an offer she could, and did, refuse.

Hawk's Last First Kiss - Would Sadie be Hawk's last first kiss?

Christmas Grump - Stuck together in her tiny house, would the Grump ruin her holiday mood?

Quin to the Rescue - Rescuing her cat from a tree was only the beginning.

A Whisper Through Time - Will Jaya choose love or peace?

Heart of a Tin Man - Can the heart-hardened Tin Man save Dorrie and her little dog too?

Also from the Lavish family

Between the Trees

Kathy Moczerniak

https://www.lavishpublishing.com/authors/kathy-moczerniak/

A beautiful coming of age with a dark side that one teenager must fight to overcome…

Beyond Kathryn Lucas' first memory of her father's tree lay a dysfunctional path of violence, heartbreak, and secrets within a family severely entrenched in the vicious cycle of abuse. A lifetime of fear drives her from her home, and the teenage girl finds refuge with an aunt and uncle determined to protect their niece.

Distressing flashbacks unravel in Kathryn's fragile mind among the turmoil encircling her as she struggles through adolescence and descends into her pain-ridden past. When the summation of her unsettling memories allows the darkness to overtake her, she becomes desperate to unearth the light.

Inspired by a true story, Kathryn must hold on tightly to those who love her, searching for her place in a world threatening to break her as she fights to overcome life's betrayals before she is deprived of her future.

The Hunter Series

Sara J. Bernhardt

https://books2read.com/HuntersTrilogySet

Jane Callahan is a reclusive, seventeen-year-old high school student dealing with the death of her beloved brother. Her home in Southern California with her mother is a constant reminder of her loss and pain. In hopes of escaping her past she moves to North Bend Oregon to live with her father, where she meets a beautiful boy named Aidan Summers.

Jane is intrigued by his looks as well as his unusual ways of attempting to get her attention. After months of uncommon conversation and frustration, an uncertain romance brews between Jane and Aidan, but Aidan has a ghastly secret that could destroy everything.

Summer Spirit Novella Series

Samantha Jacobey

https://www.lavishpublishing.com/authors/samantha-jacobey/

No one EVER had a summer romance like this... Charlie visits another plane, parallel to our own, where Summer Angels and Dark Angels battle over the fate of man. A unique twist on an old idea that will keep you guessing; will Charlie and Clarisse ever find their HEA? (New adult)

www.ingramcontent.com/pod-product-compliance
Lightning Source LLC
Chambersburg PA
CBHW032205190626
46810CB00018B/1615